Gun Storm

Deputy Jim Donovan has his fair share of worries: his brother has suffered brain damage as a result of an accident; the notorious Elroy Johnson is back in circulation, after Donovan put him away; and Martha Preston, wife of the local store keeper has been robbed and murdered.

There is temptation from Della Jordan, attractive owner of the local saloon, to quit his job and take a job on her horse ranch, but can Della be trusted? And with Stomp Cullen and his gang in town to rob the bank is there going to be any way to avoid the mighty gun storm?

Gun Storm

Corba Sunman

A Black Horse Western

ROBERT HALE · LONDON

© Corba Sunman 2013
First published in Great Britain 2013

ISBN 978-0-7198-0871-5

Robert Hale Limited
Clerkenwell House
Clerkenwell Green
London EC1R 0HT

www.halebooks.com

The right of Corba Sunman to be identified as
author of this work has been asserted by him
in accordance with the Copyright, Designs and
Patents Act 1988

Typeset by
Derek Doyle & Associates, Shaw Heath
Printed and bound in Great Britain by
CPI Antony Rowe, Chippenham and Eastbourne

ONE

The crack of a rifle shot hammered through the heavy silence in the grey mountain peaks of Colorado. Deputy Sheriff Jim Donovan heard the whine of a 44.40 slug passing his left ear and kicked his feet out of his stirrups. He dived sideways out of the saddle, dragging his Winchester from its boot as he dropped to the ground. A second slug threw dirt into his eyes. He rolled down a slope into the cover of a dry wash, and listened to the echoes of the shots drifting away across the illimitable rocky terrain.

Donovan's blue eyes were narrowed. They stung as sweat ran into them from his bronzed forehead. He listened to the fading echoes of the shots, assuming that they were being fired by the killer who had ridden into town earlier that morning and murdered Martha Preston in the general store and killed a couple of townsmen when making his escape. With only a sketchy description of the killer, Donovan had left town on the jump, picked up the killer's trail and was now hard on his heels.

Donovan lifted his head to look around. The rifle fired again, and dust flew into his eyes. He ducked and rolled to his right, observed once more and caught a glimpse of a moving Stetson on the crest above. The gun echoes faded and silence slowly returned. Donovan checked his Winchester, jacked a brass shell into the breech and pulled the butt into his shoulder. The Stetson on the rise paused and then a face showed under it as the killer looked for a target.

Donovan snapped off a shot. The Stetson flew into the air before skittering away. Gunsmoke blew into his face. The killer fell with blood showing on his forehead. Donovan held his fire as the man flopped, face down, and lay motionless. He cuffed sweat from his forehead and got to his feet, rifle ready, and went up the slope to where the man was lying.

He covered the figure as he approached, checking the description he had been given with what he could see. The man was tall, thin, aged forty or thereabouts; he wore a blue shirt and a yellow neckerchief. A horse stamped in the background and Donovan glanced up, nodding when he saw a black horse with several white spots on its hind quarters. The description tallied.

That clinched it for Donovan. He dropped to one knee beside the killer and found a wad of greenbacks in the man's breast pocket – likely stolen from the general store in Lodestone.

Donovan pushed himself to his feet. At twenty-four, he stood just over six-three. His powerful figure tipped the scales at a few ounces under two hundred pounds. He was well proportioned, lean and deadly. His blue eyes contained a brightness that spoke of grim determination. His brown hair was long, curling around his ears and at the nape of his neck. He was wearing a town suit of dark grey material, and brown shoes. A cartridge belt with filled loops was buckled around his waist, with a Colt .45 nestled in the tied-down holster. His deputy sheriff badge gleamed in the sunlight.

He leaned his Winchester against a rock and went to the horse. His search of the saddle-bags revealed nothing of interest, so Donovan led the horse to the dead man and loaded the body across the saddle. He collected his rifle. His face was expressionless as he led the horse down the slope to where his own animal was standing motionless with trailing reins.

It was a five-mile ride back to Lodestone, the little silver-mining town of some four hundred souls, where Donovan served the law under the auspices of Dan Turner, the county sheriff. Donovan thrust his rifle back into its boot, swung into the saddle and tied the reins of the black horse to his saddle-horn. He glanced at the sun and decided it would be night-fall before he got back to town. As he started the return ride he wondered what his brother Joey was doing at that moment, and hoped the youngster was not getting into trouble.

7

Lodestone was huddled at the entrance to a gorge that cut through a range of mountains in the silver-bearing area south of Moundville. The cabins and tents of the townsfolk were crowded together, straggling haphazardly on either side of the dusty trail that followed the line of least resistance all the way to Denver. The town was dwarfed by surrounding peaks.

Donovan reached the outskirts of the town as evening shadows crawled into dusty corners. Yellow lamplight was already showing at some cabin windows. The big saloon was busy – batwings creaking to and fro; strident music echoed along the street. Donovan reined up in front of the law office, stepped down from his saddle and hitched the dead man's horse to a convenient post.

The office door stood open. Sheriff Turner was sitting at his desk, busy with paperwork. Turner suffered from arthritis in his hands and feet, and could barely sit a horse these days. He had got into the habit of permitting Donovan to take over more and more of his duties. He looked up quickly when his deputy appeared.

'You ain't been gone five minutes, Jim.' Turner had turned fifty, and his short fleshy body was running to seed; grey hair sparse on the crown of his head, drooping moustache turning white. Grey eyes peered from under a screen of bushy eyebrows. He hitched up his sagging gun-belt, then leaned both hands on the desk and stifled a groan as pain racked him. He glanced sideways at Donovan, his pale eyes glinting in the lamplight. 'Did you have any luck?'

'I caught him on the first slope before Cow Creek,' Donovan replied.

'So where is he?'

'Outside – face down across his saddle.'

'You killed him!' Turner straightened.

'Had to. He ambushed me.'

'That's a pity.' Turner heaved a long, torturous sigh. 'From what I learned after you rode out, he didn't rob the store! It seems he went in just after Martha Preston was killed, saw her lying there, lost his nerve and made a run for it. Your brother Joey came out of the store behind him, yelling that Martha had been killed. Frank Pickett challenged the man as he rode out, and was shot down. Caleb Jones heard the shooting, emerged from his barber shop and was cut down without warning.'

'I don't believe this!' Donovan muttered. 'Who told you he didn't kill Mrs Preston?'

'Who else but your brother. I've put him behind bars for his own protection.' Turner picked up the cell keys and unlocked the door that gave access to the cell block. 'He's been sitting quiet as a mouse since I brought him in, and won't answer any questions.'

Donovan pushed forward as the sheriff entered the cells. He halted in mid-stride when he saw his younger brother sitting hunched on a bunk in the nearest cell. Joey Donovan was seventeen years of age; big-boned like his older brother. His boyish face, set in a mask of shock, seemed to crumple when he saw Jim.

'Why am I locked in here, Jim?' he demanded. 'I ain't done a thing! Do they think I robbed Martha?'

'Is this a joke, Dan?' asked Donovan angrily. 'Why in hell is Joey in here? Do you know what this could do to his mind? The doc said to keep him calm at all times.'

'I explained to Joey why I locked him in,' Turner said patiently. 'Heck, Jim, Mort Preston has accused Joey of killing Martha and robbing the store and he's threatening to drag him out to the nearest tree and stretch his neck. I couldn't let him run around free.'

'You know he's got the mind of a child,' Donovan scowled. 'Preston won't string him up. Unlock that door and let Joey out.'

'Joey did say he was cleaning out the storeroom when he heard raised voices in the store. He looked out and saw a man with a gunny sack on his head holding a pistol on Martha. She screamed and the man struck her on the head with the gun before going round the counter and hitting her several times more. He grabbed dough out of the till and left by the back door. Joey said he was scared and hid until the killer had gone. He was about to make a run for it when the man in the blue shirt entered the store. The man saw Martha lying behind the counter with her skull busted and ran out the front door. Joey followed him, yelling about Martha, and the guy

10

jumped into his saddle and headed out. When Frank Pickett challenged him he shot Frank and kept going. Caleb Jones heard the shooting, ran out of his shop, and collected a bullet. It's sure as hell a big mystery, Jim.'

'There ain't no doubt he killed Pickett and Jones,' Donovan observed as Turner unlocked the cell door. 'For a minute there I thought you were gonna tell me I'd got the wrong man. And I can't believe he didn't commit the robbery. Heck, I found this dough in his breast pocket.' He produced the greenbacks he had taken from the killer and handed them to the sheriff. 'He looks like a drifter, so where would he get a wad of dough from if not out of the store?'

'Ask Joey. You'll likely get more out of him.' Turner took the money, counted it and then went back into the office, grumbling to himself and massaging his left hip.

Donovan studied his brother's face. Joey had fallen down a well when he was nine years old, injuring his head and retarding his mental growth. Although he possessed the body of a young adult, he acted as if he were still a child. He was intelligent, but did not possess the maturity of his years.

'So you were cleaning out the storeroom this morning for Martha,' Donovan said. 'Tell me what happened, Joey.'

'I'm hungry, Jim. Can't we go get something to eat?'

'In a minute. I've got things to do right now that

11

can't be put off. Tell me what I wanta know and then we'll get some grub.'

'Yeah, OK. Martha asked me to help her out. You know I'm always doing odd jobs for her.'

'So what happened? You suddenly heard loud voices, huh?'

'That's right. A man was shouting. Martha screamed. I looked out the storeroom door and saw a man at the counter. He looked kind of funny because he had a gunny sack over his head, with holes cut in the front for his eyes to see through. He was holding a gun on Martha, and when she wouldn't stop screaming he batted her on the head with it. She fell down and he went behind the counter and hit her some more. Then he took the money out of the till and headed out the back door. I ducked down until he left, and was about to come out of the storeroom when another man came in from the street. I ducked down and watched him. When he saw Martha on the floor he left in a hurry. I followed him to the door and shouted for help. The man jumped on his horse and made a run for it.'

'Tell me some more about the man with the sack on his head,' Donovan encouraged.

'There ain't nothing else to tell.' Joey shook his head emphatically.

'So you saw a man in the store, wearing no clothes but with a sack over his head.'

Joey laughed. 'Hey, he had clothes on. He wouldn't walk around town naked.'

'So what was he wearing?' Donovan asked patiently.

'Miner's boots! I noticed them. Blue denim pants and a short canvas jacket.'

'What colour was the jacket?'

'Faded blue, like his pants.'

'And you can't tell me what he looked like because he was wearing a sack on his head. So what about his voice? Did you recognize that?'

Joey shook his head. 'I don't know about voices. They're all the same to me. And sometimes I don't understand what they're saying.'

'Sure, Joey. Don't worry. Think some more about what happened in the store.'

'Sure I will. I promise. Now can we get some grub?'

Donovan nodded and they went through to the front office. Turner was seated behind his desk, and grimaced when he looked up.

'Where are you gonna take Joey?' Turner demanded.

'He's got to eat,' Donovan grimaced. 'And I could do with a bite myself.'

'Sure, but bring him back afterwards. He'll be safer behind bars until we've sorted out Martha's murder.'

Donovan paused at the street door. 'Have you had a look at the killer?' he demanded.

'Not yet,' Turner shrugged. 'Leave him out there and I'll take care of him. You did good today, Jim. But watch out for Mort Preston. He's got it into his

13

head that Joey killed Martha.'

'He must be loco with grief.' Donovan shook his head, opened the door and ushered Joey outside into the shadows on the street. He paused and then stepped back into the office. 'Wait a minute, Joey,' he said. He went around the desk and jerked open the right-hand drawer. When he took out a pile of wanted dodgers, Turner looked up at him.

'What do you want them for?' he demanded.

'I'm wondering why the man I killed out by Cow Creek ran out of the store when he saw Martha dead. He acted like a man on the run from the law. He had that wad of greenbacks on him. Have you counted it? There must be a couple hundred at least.'

Turner counted the money while Donovan riffled through the dodgers. 'More than two hundred dollars,' he announced.

Donovan paused when he found a poster bearing the face of the man he had killed. 'Here he is,' he said sharply. 'Sam Rouse; wanted for bank robbery – one of Stomp Cullen's gang.'

'The hell you say!' Turner sat back in his seat. 'If he's riding with Cullen then what's he doing in town? Heck, I hope Cullen ain't coming back this way.'

'We'll soon know if he does.' Donovan put the poster on the top of the desk and returned the others to the drawer. 'Make some inquiries about Rouse around town, Sheriff,' he suggested. 'Someone might have seen him before he went into the store.'

'Sure thing. I'll look into it,' Turner said.

Donovan departed and joined Joey on the sidewalk.

'Is that man dead?' Joey asked when he saw the killer face down across the black horse.

'He sure is. Take a look at his face and tell me if it is the man you saw enter the store after Martha was killed.'

Joey walked hesitantly to the edge of the sidewalk and peered at the inert figure.

'Can you see his face?' Donovan asked.

'Not much, but it is the man I saw this morning. I'd know him anywhere. The man wearing the gunny sack, who took the money, is the one I wouldn't know again.'

'Are you telling me the truth about what happened? You didn't make it up about the man wearing the sack, did you?'

'The hell I did, Jim. That's Gospel!'

'I hope it is because I could get into a lot of trouble if you're lying. It's OK for you to change your story now, but later it wouldn't be so good. Pull yourself together over this, Joey, and lay it on the line like you really saw it.'

'How many times I got to tell you? I can't do more than say what I saw.'

'OK. I just need to make sure.'

'Can I ride your horse to the diner?' Joey demanded.

'No. I'll put it in the barn later. Come on, before I

change my mind about eating.'

They walked along the sidewalk. Donovan kept glancing around, keenly aware of the warning the sheriff had given him about Mort Preston. He wondered why the storekeeper figured that Joey had killed Martha, and realized that he would have to confront Preston, if only to put him straight about the situation.

When they reached the batwings of the Golden Slipper saloon, Joey made a lunge for the bright lights. Donovan grasped him by the shoulder and pulled him back.

'I wanta get a look at Della,' Joey protested.

'I thought you said you were hungry. If we don't get a move on the diner will be closed.'

'So you're back, Jim!' A woman's voice, pitched low, came from the darker shadows between the batwings and the nearest saloon window.

'Hi, Della,' Joey said quickly. 'We're on our way to the diner.'

Della Jordan, the proprietor of the Golden Slipper saloon, eased forward out of the shadows. She was tall and graceful, with a great figure and shoulder-length brown hair. Her dress was off-the-shoulder, a creation of green and white satin, and her shoulders and arms gleamed in the light issuing from a nearby window. The shadows did not conceal her attractive features; she was aged twenty-six.

'I've been hoping you'd get back tonight, Jim.' Della moved close to him and put a hand on his arm.

She was in love with him but he had never made a move on her so she was afraid of scaring him off. 'I need to talk to you urgently. If you're on your way to the diner you can save money by coming to eat with me – you and Joey.'

'I sure would like to, Della.' Joey pushed forward and Donovan restrained him.

'I'll see you later, Della,' Donovan said. 'When I've got Joey settled down for the night I'll come and see you. But I give you fair warning that I won't change my mind about working for you. Joey comes first, and as deputy I get time to keep an eye on him.'

'I've got a warning for you,' Della replied, 'and it's serious, Jim.'

'It always is with you. OK, I'll see you later.' Donovan propelled Joey away from the batwings.

'Hold it,' Della called. 'I daren't wait until later. It's about Elroy Johnson. He's been seen around my spread, Jim, and he could be in town now, laying for you.'

'Thanks, Della,' Donovan replied. 'I owe you a favour. I hadn't heard Johnson was out.'

'From what little I gather, I reckon he busted out,' Della said, 'and I heard he's got several men with him. So you'd better watch your step, Jim. Come and see me as soon as you can. You're gonna need some gun help to face Johnson, and I've got the men who could back you.'

'Yeah, at a price, huh? But thanks for the warning.' Donovan pushed Joey along the sidewalk in the direction of the diner.

'I like Della,' Joey said. 'She's always kind to me.'

'She's kind to a lot of folks,' Donovan replied.

Joey grumbled and tried to argue, but Donovan was adamant. When they approached the store, Joey's steps began to lag. Donovan placed a heavy hand on his shoulder and kept him moving. The door of the store was standing open and bright lamp-light issued in a shaft across the sidewalk. Several men were standing in a group before the doorway, and Donovan saw the tall, thin figure of Mort Preston, the storekeeper, facing them. He heard the mumble of angry voices, and Preston's voice sounded above all the others, shrill and furious.

'I reckon we should go along to the jail and get that halfwit out of there and string him up,' Preston was saying. 'You all know what he's like. He's loco, and shouldn't be out on the street. I reckon he killed my Martha, and he's got the store takings stashed away somewhere. He'll steal anything that ain't nailed down. I've caught him more than once taking things out of the store. Martha was good to him, but I reckon he turned on her.'

Donovan pushed Joey behind him and warned him to stay out of sight. He went forward to the rear of the townsmen and halted, shaking his head as he listened to more of Preston's tirade. He saw that Preston was holding a double-barrelled shotgun.

'Hey, Mort,' he called. 'What are you trying to do, talk up a lynching against my brother? He's only a kid and don't know right from wrong. Why don't you shut up and go back in the store? Leave the law dealing to us. We'll get Martha's killer.'

Preston came forward a step, peering over the crowd.

'So you come back, huh?' he demanded. 'And I'll bet you didn't catch that killer.'

'I got him face down across his saddle outside the law office right now.'

There was a ripple of voices, and the next instant the men around Donovan went running along the sidewalk to look at the dead man. Preston remained motionless, and the muzzle of his shotgun lifted to gape at Donovan's chest.

'What makes you think Joey had anything to do with Martha's death?' Donovan asked.

'That story he gave about a man with a sack on his head is one of his tall yarns.' Preston took a fresh grip on his gun. 'That kid brother of yours is a danger to everyone. Heck, he almost burned down the livery barn a couple of weeks ago.'

'He said he didn't do that and I believe him.' Anger edged Donovan's tone. 'What have you got against him that you wanta see him lynched? You should be fired up about getting whoever killed your wife. You won't see justice done by accusing Joey.'

'You would stick up for him,' said Preston thickly. A couple of metallic clicks sounded as he cocked the hammers on the shotgun. Donovan felt a cold pang stab through his chest.

19

'Point that shotgun someplace else, Preston,' he said sharply. 'You're piling up trouble for yourself.'

The overwrought storekeeper lifted the butt of the shotgun to his shoulder. Donovan looked into the twin barrels of the fearsome weapon and held his breath as silence closed in about them. Joey moved impatiently behind Donovan. Time seemed to stand still, and Donovan was aware that his life was hanging on the pressure of Preston's trigger finger.

TWO

'Mort, what in hell are you playing at? Are you fixing to shoot Jim?' Sheriff Turner edged into sight from the shadows along the sidewalk and came to stand in front Donovan. 'Put down that damn gun. I wanta know why you're picking on Joey.'

'That damn halfwit,' Preston declared. 'He killed Martha.'

'You're talking through the back of your neck,' Turner replied. 'Joey is an important witness, and he's only a kid. So put down that gun before I get good and mad.'

Preston stood motionless, and the silence about them intensified. Donovan breathed slowly, just waiting for the next move. There was nothing a man could do except pray when he was staring into a shotgun from a few feet.

'I'm waiting, Mort,' Turner prompted.

The storekeeper lowered his gun and turned

abruptly. Donovan heard Turner sigh with relief as Preston limped into the store and slammed the door.

'I'll keep an eye on him,' Turner said. 'It's only natural he's upset about Martha.'

'Just a minute, Dan,' Donovan said as the sheriff turned away. 'I've been told that Elroy Johnson has been seen around. Have you heard anything?'

'The hell you say! No I ain't picked up on that. Heck he should be in prison for at least another seven years.'

'Della warned me to watch out for him. She knows he threatened to kill me when I sent him to prison. If he is back then he must have escaped, huh?'

'I'll check it out.' Turner moved off. 'Keep your eyes open, Jim.'

Donovan grimaced and continued towards the diner, a hand on Joey's shoulder.

'That was bad what Mr Preston did, huh?' Joey demanded. 'I thought he was gonna shoot you, Jim.'

'For a moment back there, so did I,' Donovan replied.

They entered the diner and had a good meal. Donovan was gripped with impatience. He wanted to get back to Della and learn more about Elroy Johnson. A local badman, Johnson had caused endless trouble with his lawless ways – running a gang to rustle cattle, steal horses and work his way up through a whole list of crimes until he had bitten off more than he could chew by robbing a stage coach. A passenger had recognized his voice and reported his suspicion to the law office. Donovan had taken a posse out to Johnson's run-down ranch, and caught Johnson and his gang in the act of sharing out the contents of the stolen Wells Fargo box.

'Why'd Mr Preston think I killed Martha?'

'You were in the store at the time, and his ideas don't run far in any direction. Forget about it now and get on with eating. I got things to do this evening.'

'Why do I have to sleep behind bars? Do you think I did something wrong today?'

'No. But you saw how Mort Preston wanted to shoot you, and there could be other men around who might blame you for something you didn't do. You'll be safer in jail, Joey.'

When they finished their meal, Donovan took Joey back to the law office. The black horse with the killer's body across the saddle was gone, and Donovan's horse nudged him when he patted its nose.

'I'll take care of you in a minute,' Donovan said, patting the animal's neck.

He unlocked the law office door, ushered Joey inside and locked him in a cell.

'I don't like it in here, Jim,' Joey complained. 'I liked our cabin better.'

'I told you why you've got to stay in here. Now settle down and get some sleep. Is there anything I can get you before I go?'

23

'No.' Joey stretched out on the bunk and turned his back.

Donovan shook his head and returned to the front office. He stood for a moment considering all that had occurred during the long day. There were big questions on his mind. Who had killed and robbed Martha Preston? What was Sam Rouse doing in town that morning? Had Rouse and the killer been working together? He departed, locked the street door and swung into his saddle to ride along the street to the livery barn.

The main street was lively but the rest of the town was quiet and in deep shadow. The piano music coming from the Golden Slipper echoed loudly. The big saloon was crowded as usual, and he thought about Della Jordan as he continued along the street. Della had been trying for weeks to talk him into leaving his law job and take a job with her – running the horse ranch she owned fifteen miles south of Lodestone. So far he had held out against her, but she had lately increased her offer, and now he had half a mind to accept the job because Joey would be on a ranch instead of running wild around town.

He dismounted outside the big open barn door and waited while his horse drank its fill from a nearby water trough. The surrounding shadows were dense. A lantern was alight inside the barn, but its feeble glow did little to disperse the darkness. When the horse was satisfied he led it into the barn, then found an empty stall and took care of its needs. He poured crushed oats into the manger and then fetched a forkful of hay. As he left the stall he heard a furtive sound off to his left, from deeper inside the barn.

He dropped to one knee and drew his pistol. Full alertness had him searching the shadows with narrowed gaze, and he wondered if his nerves were getting the better of him. When the sound was not repeated he started to his feet, and a ribbon of orange muzzle flame speared through the shadows from the rear of the barn. The echoing crash of a pistol shot blasted like thunder and a bullet splintered through the woodwork of the stall close to his left shoulder. He threw himself flat, gun cocked and ready for action.

Donovan's eyes were dazzled by the gun flash and he blinked rapidly. He strained his ears, but all he could hear was the hammering echoes of the shot. His horse stamped nervously, one hoof narrowly missing his shoulder. He squirmed aside, and then crawled out of the stall on his hands and knees. Straw crackled as he moved, and the pistol fired again, filling the barn with discordant thunder. Donovan closed his eyes, dropped flat and rolled under the bottom rail of the stall.

He got up and ran for cover behind a grain bin. A bullet smacked into its side. He gained his feet and dived into an unoccupied stall, barely able to see in the feeble glow emitted by the solitary lamp high on a post. He waited then, gun poised and finger trembling with anticipation on the trigger. The gun echoes faded and he listened intently for unnatural sound.

An ear-splitting yell startled him and he ducked, but no shooting erupted. Then a jeering voice called out.

'I got you dead to rights, Donovan. It's me, Elroy Johnson. I told you I'd come back and get you. I've been waiting all day, and now I'm gonna kill you.'

Donovan did not reply. As the echoes of Johnson's voice faded, a stark thought flashed into his mind: Johnson was back, and Martha Preston had been robbed and killed by a man wearing a hood. Had Johnson been responsible?

Donovan eased forward in the direction from whence the shots had come, determined to take Johnson alive.

Johnson did not speak again, and the barn was so quiet that Donovan thought the badman had pulled out. He paused, thumbed a cartridge from a loop in his belt and tossed it ahead, aiming for a post. The slight sound made by the cartridge striking the post brought an immediate response from Johnson. His gun blasted three times, and hot lead hammered across the barn. Donovan moved forward on his stomach, and when the echoes died he caught the sound of Johnson reloading his pistol.

Donovan got to his feet and went forward quickly. He saw a figure rear up out of the shadows and fired a shot, aiming for a shoulder. Johnson yelled as the slug hit him. He spun around, trying to bring his gun into action. Donovan fired again, aiming for a wounding shot, needing answers to the questions nagging him.

Johnson's gun flew from his hand. He lunged for it. Donovan ran forward and slammed his gun barrel against Johnson's head as the badman's fingers closed around the fallen gun. Johnson fell face down and remained inert. Donovan kicked the pistol aside before bending over Johnson. He turned the man over and saw a dark splotch of blood on the shirt covering the left shoulder.

Donovan holstered his gun and grasped Johnson's right arm, dragging him out of the barn and dropping him in the big doorway. He looked around, and saw figures coming along the street, attracted by the shooting. He examined Johnson more closely, and decided that he would survive.

Sheriff Turner was one of the first to arrive. He was holding his gun, and paused, his face showing surprise when he saw the huddled body at Donovan's feet.

'Who is he?' Turner demanded. 'Is it Johnson?'

'It is.' Donovan expelled his pent-up breath in a long sigh. 'He was waiting inside the barn for me.'

'Is he dead?'

'The hell he is. I've got some questions for him.'

'He reckoned on killing you.' Turner laughed harshly. 'You'd think he'd have learned a lesson when you arrested him three years ago. Stay with him while I fetch Doc Hardy.'

'I had a thought when Johnson was shooting at me,' Donovan mused. 'I'm wondering if he robbed and killed Martha.'

Turner paused and looked at Donovan. 'He's a known badman, and he was around. I think you've hit the nail on the head, Jim. We'll grill him when we get him behind bars. I'll be back in a minute.'

Donovan stood over the unconscious badman. Several townsmen arrived and wanted to know what had happened. Turner returned with Doc Hardy, who dropped to his knees beside Johnson and examined him. Hardy was in his fifties, tall, lean, with greying hair, and had seen it all in his thirty years in the West. He got to his feet and turned to Donovan.

'Are you OK, Jim?' he asked.

'You don't think a two-bit punk like Johnson could beat a man like my deputy, do you, Doc?' Turner demanded.

'I'm OK, Doc,' Donovan said. 'Will he live?'

'Barring complications, his life is not in danger. Can you get him along to my office?'

Turner ordered four of the townsmen to pick up Johnson and take him along to the doc's place. Donovan walked along the street with the sheriff, but paused when he reached the batwings of the Golden Slipper.

'You can handle Johnson, Dan,' he said. 'I need a drink, and I wanta talk to Della. She might be able to fill me in on more details about Johnson. I'll see you back at the jail.'

'Take your time, Jim. You've done more than your share today. I'll handle Johnson. But I'll leave you to question him.'

Donovan entered the saloon, which was crowded. He saw Della standing at the bar. Her face was showing the drift of her thoughts; brooding. Her lips were compressed, but she brightened when she saw Donovan. She came to him quickly. The bright lamp-light of the garish saloon revealed her attractiveness. Her forehead was smooth and unblemished; the skin of her face pure and white.

'That shooting, Jim,' she said. 'Was it Johnson after you?'

'Yeah, and he made a mistake. He's on his way to the doc's office with a bullet in him. What can you tell me about him, Della? How'd you know he was back? Where'd you get your news from?'

She smiled. 'You know I won't talk about my contacts. If word got out that I couldn't keep a secret I wouldn't hear another thing. I come up against all types in this business, Jim. Some men like to talk when they've had a drink or two, and most of them brag about what they've been doing. I listen, and never forget a thing.'

'So do you know when Johnson was first seen in town?' Donovan cut in.

'Is that important?'

'It is to me. I think he might have committed

murder and robbery today, so I've got to check him out, and I need all the help I can get.'

'Martha Preston?' Della swallowed nervously as she spoke. 'Do you think Johnson robbed the store and killed her?'

'I'm not thinking anything at the moment. I have a crime to investigate, and Johnson is a known badman so I have to run him through the mill. So what can you tell me about him? As far as we know, he's still got another seven years to serve in prison. If he broke out of the Pen then we'll hear about it, but so far there's been no word.'

Della shook her head, her expression impassive. 'Johnson was spotted near my ranch yesterday. Frank Doane rode in this afternoon to tell me; Johnson spells trouble wherever he's at. That's why I asked you to come and talk to me.'

'You should have passed on this news the minute you got it,' Donovan said heavily. 'It might have saved Martha's life.'

A shadow crossed Della's face. 'I didn't think there was any need for haste,' she said. 'I hope Johnson didn't kill her. I'd never be able to live with the knowledge that I could have prevented that poor woman's death by telling you earlier.'

'There are a lot of bad things I have to live with,' Donovan retorted.

'Come into my office and have a drink,' Della invited.

'Only if you promise not to nag me about coming

30

to work for you,' he countered. 'You know I'm tied down with Joey. He takes a lot of watching these days, and there's no one I can leave him with. That's why I'm sticking to law dealing. The sheriff is good enough to let me watch out for Joey when I'm on duty.'

'I need you working for me, Jim,' she said. 'I'm expanding my business interests all the time and good men are hard to find. I'll make it worth your while, and also do something about Joey. Think about it, will you?'

'I've done nothing but think about it.' He shook his head. 'You're complicating my life, Della. I had it all planned out, and now you've got me thinking in other directions. Heck, I just don't know what to do.'

'Take a chance and throw in with me. You'll never regret it.'

'Like I said, it's not that simple. Give me a break, Della. Lay off. Look, I'd better get moving. We'll have that drink another time. I've still got a lot to do before I can call it a day.'

He turned on his heel and headed for the batwings. Della called after him but he ignored her and kept going. Then he paused at the swing doors and looked back.

'When Johnson was seen near your place was he alone?' he demanded.

'I don't know. I heard only that he was seen. Is it important?'

'It could be a matter of life or death,' he responded.

He left the saloon, and a sigh escaped him as he paused on the shadowed sidewalk. An indistinct shadow was coming across the street and he instinctively dropped a hand to his holstered pistol.

'Is that you, Donovan?' a man called.

'Yeah,' he replied. He did not recognize the voice and came to full alertness, drawing and cocking his pistol.

The next instant gun flame stabbed at him as the man opened fire, and bullets thudded against the front of the saloon. Donovan dived low and rolled off the sidewalk into the street. His gun hand lifted and he aimed at the man, now wreathed in gunsmoke. He triggered two shots, his ears protesting at the noise. He screwed up his eyes against drifting smoke. The man turned to run for cover but began staggering uncertainly, and, as Donovan lifted his gun for another shot the man pitched forward on to his face and lay still.

Thinking the spate was over, Donovan began to arise, but then two more guns opened fire from the sidewalk to his right. He dropped flat as slugs smacked into the dust around him. Muzzle flame concealed his attackers. Donovan rolled in under the edge of the sidewalk and steeled himself to continue the fight. He had no idea who was attacking him, but questions could wait. Right now he had to gain the upper hand. He thrust his gun up over the edge of the sidewalk, fired two shots in the general direction of the two men, and then sprang to his feet and began fighting in earnest.

The noise of the shooting echoed around the street. Donovan sweated as he squeezed off at the two figures. Slugs were striking around him. A nearby awning post splintered. The attackers were firing haphazardly, deluging him with fire, and all their shots were wide. Donovan directed his shots into his targets.

One man dropped out of the fight instantly. The second man retreated to the nearest alley and dived into it. He fired two shots from cover, and then the shooting faded and silence returned. Donovan wrinkled his nose at the stench of gunsmoke. He reloaded the empty chambers of his pistol before moving forward. A couple of heads were showing at the batwings of the saloon, and then the swing doors were pushed open and men emerged to investigate the shooting.

Donovan went to the man lying in the street, checked him, and found him to be dead – a stranger. He went to the man prone on the sidewalk as townsmen came pushing around the corpse to stand and stare and talk excitedly. The second man was dead also – another stranger. There was no sign of the third man. Donovan looked into the shadowed alley and then stepped quickly to one side into cover. There was no reaction from the darkness. The third man had departed.

Sheriff Turner came along the street and paused in the lamplight issuing from the saloon. His gun was in his hand. He looked around. Donovan called to him.

'What happened?' Turner demanded.

Donovan made a report. Turner moved his feet as if impatient to go elsewhere.

'What in hell is going on, Jim?' he demanded.

'Yesterday we had a peaceful town here,' Donovan replied. 'When I got up at dawn this morning I was feeling lucky to be alive. Since then it's been like a nightmare.'

'You rode out after the killer, and got him.' Turner shook his head. 'Then Elroy Johnson turned up out of the blue and tried to kill you. Now this has happened. Can you tell me what is going on?'

'I sure wish I could.' Donovan shook his head, smiling mirthlessly. 'I've got no more idea than you, Dan.'

'Johnson was talking nineteen to the dozen when I stuck him behind bars. He reckons they turned him loose from the big prison for good behaviour. Maybe he thought I'd fall for that. You should speak to him now. He's ready to talk the hind leg off a mule.'

'He'll clam up the minute I mention his past.' Donovan grimaced. 'Get this mess cleaned up, Dan, and I'll start in on Johnson.'

'Get tough with him,' Turner advised. 'He's crowing like a Sunday rooster.'

Donovan shook his head as he went on to the law

office. He didn't like the way the wind was blowing. It seemed that big trouble was settling in around this little community, and he began to wonder what was behind it.

THREE

The sheriff had left the lamp alight in the front office, and Donovan entered and locked the door behind him. He took the cell keys from the right-hand drawer in the paper-strewn desk and went into the cell block. A lamp was burning on a shelf beside the door, casting a dim glow across the row of four cells and the back door. Donovan looked into Joey's cell and saw his brother sitting on his bunk, gripping the bars that separated his cell from the adjoining one – in which Elroy Johnson was detained – chatting happily to the badman, who was propped up on his bunk, his left arm in a sling and his shoulder heavily bandaged.

Johnson was white-faced and badly shocked but grinning, although his smile vanished when he saw Donovan. Joey jumped up from his bunk and came to his cell door, grinning happily at his brother.

'What the hell is going on?' Donovan demanded.

'I'm getting to know Joey,' Johnson said. His lean

face showed the rigours of his past three years in the big prison, and his brown eyes glittered as he took in Donovan's appearance. 'You're looking a lot better than me,' he observed. 'What are you gonna do about me?'

'Put you back where you belong.' Donovan smiled grimly. 'You tried to kill me, Johnson. You didn't learn a damn thing from before.'

'The hell I did! If I'd only half-tried you would be dead right now. I wanted to throw a scare into you, that's all. I learned my lesson in jail, and I don't wanta go back there.'

'Then you should have stayed away from Lodestone. What's the big attraction here, anyway?' Donovan glanced at his brother. Joey was hanging on to every word being spoken. 'From what I hear you didn't ride in alone, Johnson. What bunch have you tied in with? I was shot at by three strangers after I arrested you in the barn. One of them got away in an alley, but the other two are lying in the street, waiting for the undertaker. Were they your friends?'

'I came back here alone.' Johnson shook his head. 'I'm finished with the life I knew before you put me away. I'm going straight after this.'

Donovan laughed sardonically. 'That'll be the day – straight back to prison, you mean.' He paused, and then asked quickly, 'Who is Sam Rouse?'

Johnson's eyes flickered but his face remained expressionless. 'Rouse,' he mused, shaking his head. 'I can't say I know the name. Who is he?'

Donovan did not reply. He knew Johnson was lying. He looked at the clothes Johnson was wearing – riding boots, grey whipcord pants, and a red shirt – nothing like the clothes Joey had described on Martha's killer.

'Where were you staying in town?' Donovan asked.

'I slept in the hayloft at the livery barn last night, and tonight it looks like I'll be staying right here. But I don't mind where I sleep these days. Anywhere is better than a cell in the big prison.' Johnson laughed, evidently relieved by the change of direction in Donovan's questioning. 'What's your brother doing behind bars, huh? Can't you find him a better place to sleep?'

'Tell me your movements early this morning,' Donovan said.

'Sure. I got nothing to hide. I left the stable around seven and had breakfast in the diner. After that I mooched around town looking for a job, although I don't expect you to believe that.'

'Where were you when that shooting took place on the street?'

'I can tell you that OK. I remember hearing the commotion. I was talking to Abe Williams, the freighter man, hoping to get a job with him. But he recognized me from three years ago so it was no dice. When we heard the shots we walked into the street and stood there, watching what was going on. I saw you take out after the man who did the shooting.'

'The freight line office is next to the general

store,' Donovan mused. 'I think you were in the store with the intention of picking up some easy dough. Martha Preston was there alone, and she screamed when you asked for money, so you beat her over the head, stole the cash and then went out the back door. Did you head straight into the freight office for an alibi?'

'The hell I did! What are you trying to do, pin that on me? You got the killer, didn't you?' Johnson grimaced as he looked squarely into Donovan's eyes.

'At the time I thought I got the guy who killed Frank Pickett and Caleb Jones on the street after he had murdered Martha and robbed the store, but when I brought his body back to town I learned from a witness that someone else did for Martha – someone who looked like you, Johnson.'

'I didn't say Johnson was the man in the store,' Joey cut in. 'He ain't anything like the man I saw. Why are you lying, Jim?'

'Don't worry, kid. He's just trying to set me up,' said Johnson, laughing.

Donovan unlocked the door of Joey's cell. 'Come on out of there,' he ordered. 'If you can't keep your mouth shut then I'll put you where you can't hear anything.'

He released Joey and took him into the small rear kitchen. The door of a single cell off the kitchen stood open, and Donovan locked Joey inside.

'I don't like this cell,' Joey complained. 'I can't talk to Elroy from here.'

'Stay away from him, and don't tell him anything about what you saw in the store, or anywhere else, for that matter. Now get on that bunk and try to sleep.'

Donovan left his brother complaining and went into the front office. Someone was knocking at the street door, and Donovan heaved a sigh as he opened it. Abe Williams, the owner of the livery barn and the local freight line, came forward. Donovan stepped back to permit him entry. Williams was tall and thin, in his early fifties. His taut face was tense, his dark eyes gleaming with suppressed excitement.

'Have you come to complain about the shooting in your barn, Abe?' Donovan asked.

'No. It's a pity you didn't kill Johnson when you had the chance. He came into my freight office this morning asking for a job. The damn nerve of the thieving pack rat! Can you imagine me sending him to one of the big mines to pick up a silver shipment?'

Donovan nodded. 'You were in your office at the time the store was robbed. Did you hear anything suspicious? I was told Martha screamed when the robber asked for money.'

Williams shook his head. 'I never heard a thing. The stamp mills of the Perkins mine are near to my place, and I can't hear anything when they're crushing ore.'

'Did you see anyone acting suspiciously at that time?'

'The only man I saw about that time was Johnson. We were talking when the shooting that killed Pickett and Jones took place.'

'How long was Johnson with you before the shooting?'

Williams rubbed his chin. 'Five minutes, I guess.'

'What was his manner when you saw him?'

Williams' eyes widened as he grasped the drift of Donovan's questions. 'Say, do you think Johnson killed Martha? Jeez, the nerve of that guy! He knocked over the store and then sauntered into my place asking for a job.'

'I'm not thinking anything like that,' Donovan shook his head. 'I'm checking facts. So what was Johnson's manner like when you saw him?'

'No different to how he always looks, although I haven't seen him in more than three years.'

'Can you remember how was he dressed?'

'Blue denim jacket and pants, I guess. That's what everyone wears around here. Now that's enough about Johnson. I want to tell you about two men who came into the livery barn about fifteen minutes ago. Hard men – long riders, I reckon. They put up their horses, and said they'd pick them up later. One of them struck me as looking like I'd seen him before, so I followed the pair of them to see what they were up to. They went into the Golden Slipper by the back door, and I came straight here to tell you because one of them looked mighty like Stomp Cullen, the outlaw.

'The hell you say!' Donovan went to the sheriff's desk, jerked open a drawer and took out the pile of

41

dog-eared Wanted dodgers. He skimmed through them, found the one he was looking for and placed it on the desk so Williams could see it.

Williams pounced on it and moved closer to the lamp to study it. 'Yeah,' he said, 'I never forget a face. I was in the bank in Moundville last year when Cullen and his gang robbed it. That damned bandit took my father's gold watch off me. I'd sure like to get it back.'

'Is he the man you saw going in the back of the saloon?' Donovan demanded.

'That's right. What are you gonna do about it?'

'I'll take a look there now.' Donovan drew his Colt and checked it.

'Heck, there's gonna be more shooting! Cullen won't give in without a fight. You better get some help before you brace him.'

Williams departed quickly, not wanting to be asked for his help. Donovan went out to the sidewalk, locked the street door and set off for the saloon. His thoughts were fast moving as he considered the situation. The two men he had killed earlier were strangers but he wondered if they were a part of Cullen's gang or tied in with Johnson. But if they were with Cullen then why had they come into town to shoot up the local law? Usually, badmen did not advertise their presence.

Had Johnson thrown in with Cullen? It was obvious Johnson had escaped from prison, where he had been serving ten years. And where did Sam

Rouse, who had killed Pickett and Jones, fit into the business? He had entered the store almost before Martha's killer left, and when he was challenged on his way out of town he gunned down two men. Why had he done so if he had not killed Martha?

Donovan continued to the saloon. Nothing was stirring around the street, although he was half expecting trouble to leap out at him from of the shadows. He shouldered through the swing doors and approached the bar. Hatton, the bartender, came to serve him.

'Della says in future all your drinks are on the house,' Hatton said. He was wearing a white apron over a town suit and had a black string tie around his thick neck. Forty years old, he was short and fleshy, his face shining clean; blue eyes clear and alert.

'Then I'll have to come in more often,' Donovan grinned although his lips were stiff. 'Give me a beer.' He looked around the saloon for Della but she was not present. 'Where's the lovely lady?'

'She was called to her office about half an hour ago and I ain't seen her since.' Hatton set a glass of foaming beer in front of Donovan and moved away.

Donovan drained the glass and then went to Della's office. He knocked on the door with his left hand, his gun hand down close to the butt of his holstered weapon. He was half-convinced that he would find two outlaws with Della, although he could not even guess at the business she might be engaged in with an outlaw gang boss. He heard her call out an invitation to enter and, cautiously, he opened the door.

'Hello, Jim.' Della was alone, seated at her desk, and she got to her feet and came to stand in front of Donovan. Although she smiled, her face looked as if she was carrying all the troubles of the world on her slim shoulders. 'I didn't expect to see you again this evening,' she remarked.

'It's business, Della.' He looked into her depthless blue eyes and wondered what was going through her mind. 'I've had a report that two men entered the saloon by the back door about half an hour ago; one of them looked pretty much like Stomp Cullen, the outlaw.'

Shock appeared in Della's eyes, and Donovan heard the catch of her breath. The intangible scent of her perfume wafted into his nostrils and he held his breath until it faded. She looked very attractive in the stark lamplight, and he steeled himself against her. If he had not had Joey to care for he would have allowed his feelings for her to come to the forefront of his mind.

'I don't know what it's all about,' he went on hurriedly, 'but I have to check. Have you had two hardcases in here this evening?'

'I certainly have not.' Her voice was suddenly flat and hard. 'Who gave you that information, Jim? Is someone out to make trouble for me?'

'Like you, I can't reveal my contacts.' He shifted his feet uneasily, not liking her reaction and reading bad things into it. 'I checked the saloon when I came in and didn't see anyone looking like Cullen. But I can't think of any reason why my informant should make a false statement so I have to do my duty.'

'Feel free to take the place apart, if you feel so inclined,' she said sharply. The friendliness was gone from her shimmering eyes and her lips had pulled into a thin, uncompromising line. She made an effort to pull herself together and then forced a harsh laugh. 'I don't have time for this kind of thing,' she declared. 'There are malicious people around town who would like nothing better than to cause me grief.'

'OK. I'll take your word, Della. Don't get hot under the collar. I'm not accusing you of anything. It's my job to go for any badmen who show up.'

'I'm sorry, Jim. I've got a lot on my mind right now. There's been trouble out at the ranch for some time. That's why I've been trying to get you to give up your badge and work for me. I need a strong man out there, someone I can trust.'

'Why haven't you told me about it? How can I do anything to help if you keep it to yourself? What's happened?'

'Someone is stealing horses. I've lost about sixty that I was getting together as remounts for the army.'

'And have you reported the theft to the sheriff?'

'I thought I could handle it – or at least have my crew at the ranch handle it. But it's got worse, and that's why I thought of putting you out there in charge. There's nothing you can't handle.'

'I'm not surprised there's trouble, with Elroy Johnson back in town. He was always stealing horses and cattle before we put him away.'

'It would take more than Johnson to cause my trouble,' Della replied.

'There's only one way to stop horse stealing,' Donovan mused. 'I'll ride out to your place tomorrow and take a look around. As it happens I need to check on my own place. I haven't been out that way in a couple of months. I'll take Joey with me. He always likes to visit the ranch.'

'Aren't you too busy with the trouble around town?' Della went back to her seat behind the desk and picked up a bottle of whiskey. 'Will you have a drink with me?'

He shook his head. 'No thanks. I'd better get back to the office and see what I can wring out of Johnson.' He turned to the door, opened it and then paused in the doorway. 'You look like you've got a real bad problem on your mind, Della, and if you don't level with me then I can't help you.'

He departed, leaving her gazing after him, and went through the saloon to pause just inside the batwings. He dropped his hand to his gun butt before easing through the doors and stepping quickly to one side on the sidewalk. He pushed his back against the wall and looked around for trouble. A long sigh escaped him when nothing untoward occurred. The street was silent and still, the shadows impenetrable. He drew a deep breath and some of the tension seeped out of him, but he knew that the situation was beginning to get to him, and he was well aware that one of the ambushers who had struck at him earlier on the street had got clean away.

He walked back to the jail, keeping close to the front walls of the buildings to stay in the shadows. As he passed the door of the darkened gun shop, set back some three feet from the line of the front windows, he heard leather scraping on the ground as someone moved forward out of the blackness surrounding the shop door. He stepped to his right before whirling around, caught a faint movement in the doorway, and instinctively raised his left hand to ward off a blow.

The end of a hard object, probably a pickaxe handle, struck him in the stomach, knocking the wind out of him. He groaned and fell to his knees, drawing his Colt, but before he could bring the weapon into action the heavy object rose quickly and then slammed against his head. It was as if the gun shop had fallen in on him. Lights flared in his brain; pain stabbed through his skull, and before he could take it all in, a black cloud descended on him and he fell forward on to his face.

He did not lose consciousness, though, and had enough sense left to try and squirm away from another blow. He twisted, ducked and half-rolled, fighting against the descending darkness swamping his brain, and when the heavy object struck again at his head he had managed to get his left shoulder up to deflect the blow. Raw pain blazed through his shoulder and neck and he lost his grip on the pistol. He twisted to his left and lunged forward on his knees, butting his attacker in the stomach. The man grunted and fell on top of him. Donovan grabbed at him with eager hands. His left hand seized on the weapon the man was holding – a pickaxe handle – and he clung to it.

Donovan shook his head to clear it of the fog befuddling his brain, and a wave of dizziness assailed him. He threw his right fist into the area where he expected the man's head to be, and felt the satisfactory crack of his knuckles against a jawline. The man fell backwards, dragging Donovan with him. Donovan threw another punch, felt his assailant's nose crunch and then swarmed up and lunged close, his right knee lifting to the man's stomach. He secured a hold on one of the man's upper arms, pulled him close, and then slammed his head forward in a vicious butt.

The man relaxed instantly. Donovan dropped his right hand to the man's waist, felt a gun belt and snaked his hand around to grasp the holstered weapon. He drew it clear and held it as he pushed the man away. He forced himself to his knees, breathing heavily, his senses reeling. He staggered to his feet, leaving the man lying motionless.

Donovan almost overbalanced when he bent to grasp the man's collar. He shifted his feet quickly, dragged the inert man out of the shadows of the doorway and dropped him on the sidewalk. The gleam of a nearby lantern illuminated the upturned features. The man was a stranger. Donovan leaned against a wall and drew a deep breath. By degrees his head settled down and his senses ceased to spin. He watched his assailant, saw signs of returning consciousness and stirred the man with a boot.

'OK,' he said loudly. 'Get up.'

The man got to his hands and knees, and remained in that position. Donovan grasped him by the scruff of the neck and dragged him to his feet. He rammed the muzzle of the pistol into the man's stomach.

'Who are you?' Donovan demanded. 'Why did you attack me?'

The man did not reply, but suddenly burst into a frenzy of activity. He grabbed Donovan's gun wrist and forced the muzzle of the pistol away from his body. The weapon exploded raucously and the bullet thudded into the sidewalk. Donovan grasped the man by the front of his shirt and swung the pistol. The long barrel slammed against the man's left temple and he dropped to the sidewalk without a sound.

Donovan waited until the man regained his senses. When his eyes opened, Donovan again ordered him to rise. He stepped back out of arm's length as the man complied, and then urged him to head for the jail, following behind with his gun levelled. The man was unsteady, but did not attempt to offer more resistance. When they reached the law office door, Donovan was surprised to see it standing half open. He pushed the man across the threshold and followed closely. He saw that the door leading to the cells was ajar, and thrust his prisoner against it.

The door swung wide and Donovan peered inside. His startled gaze swept along the line of cells and a pang stabbed through him when he saw Johnson's cell was empty. . . .

FOUR

Donovan stared in disbelief at Johnson's empty cell, and then thought of Joey. He grasped his prisoner by the scruff of the neck, thrust him into a cell, and slammed the door. The key was in the lock and he turned it and then withdrew it before running through to the kitchen. He pulled up short at sight of the cell door standing open. Joey was gone. He went back to the cell block and confronted his prisoner.

'Why did you jump me?' he demanded. 'You were waiting for me along the street. Was it to keep me out of here while Johnson was busted loose?'

'Go to hell!' The man sneered, and grimaced in pain when Donovan reached through the bars of cell door to grab a handful of his shirt, and jerked him forward, smashing his face against the bars.

Donovan thrust him away. 'What's your name?' he demanded as the man fell to the floor. 'I reckon you're one of the three men who ambushed me earlier.'

'I told you where to go,' the man replied.

Donovan took the cells keys into the front office and dumped them on the desk. He sat down, opened a drawer of the desk and once more took out the stack of wanted dodgers. Skimming through them, he came to the face of the man he had arrested, and read the details. His name was Noll Watson, a known member of the Cullen gang. Donovan leaned back in the chair, his mind flitting over the day's events. Cullen was supposed to have been seen entering the back door of Della's saloon and Abe Williams had come into the office to report Cullen's presence, but had the warning been given with the intention of getting the lawmen out of the office while Cullen's gang broke into the jail?

Donovan's thoughts roved on. Had Della lied to him about not seeing Cullen? He heaved a sigh, unable to believe Della could be mixed up with a gang of outlaws. And would Abe Williams have come into the law office to lie deliberately about seeing Cullen entering the rear of the saloon?

Donovan went back into the cells. In the back of his mind was a niggling thought about Joey. He could understand Johnson being busted out, but why would anyone want to take Joey along? He paused at the door of Watson's cell. The man had dragged himself on to the bunk and was stretched out, both hands to his battered face.

'OK, Watson,' he said. 'I got you dead to rights. So you run with the Cullen gang, and that's why you tried to take me. I heard Cullen was in town tonight, and while I was out hunting him he came in here and busted Johnson loose. But he made a bad mistake taking my brother along. And you'll be in big trouble if you don't tell me where they've gone. Give it to me straight because if anything bad happens to my kid brother then I'll take you apart bit by bit.'

'You got the wrong man. My name ain't Watson, and I never heard of Cullen.'

Donovan stifled a sigh. He glanced around the cell block, and noticed that the side door to an alley was standing slightly ajar. He drew his gun and ran to the door, jerked it wide and looked around outside. The alley was dark. He went for a lamp and took it outside, lifting it high to chase away the darkness. But there was nothing to see. The outlaws and Johnson were gone, and Joey was with them.

He moved along the alley to the back lots, and at the rear of the cell block he saw hoof prints in the dust. He dropped to one knee, his experienced gaze searching the bare ground. Four horses had stood together for some considerable time, and he saw that they had set out eventually across the back lots. He went back into the cell block and bolted the door.

A figure moved into the cells from the front office and Donovan reached for his gun; jerked it from its holster. He halted the movement when he recognized the sheriff. Turner was unsteady on his feet. He looked as if he'd been in the bar lubricating his insides.

'I've got some checking to do,' Donovan said. 'Our prisoners have been busted out and I wanta get them back. I'm gonna start looking for them right now.'

Donovan went to the street door. He paused and looked back at the sheriff. 'I'll start with Della. Abe Williams came in and told me he saw a man who looked like Stomp Cullen entering the saloon by the back door.'

Turner shook his head and sat down at the desk. Donovan departed.

He went to the saloon and entered quickly. The bar was crowded, and Della was standing about halfway along it, talking to the bartender. Donovan strode to her side and grasped her arm. She was startled and looked up at him quickly.

'Jim,' she gasped, 'I didn't expect to see you again this evening. What's wrong?'

'Let's go talk in your office,' he rapped, tugging her away from the bar.

Della accompanied him without hesitation and led the way into the office.

'What's happened?' she demanded.

'I'm wondering if you know,' Donovan replied. 'The man you said you hadn't seen in here, Cullen, was busy busting Elroy Johnson out of jail while I was asking you about him. Joey was in a cell for safe keeping, and they took him along with them when they rode out.'

'Joey?' A shadow crossed Della's pale features. 'Why would they want him along?'

'As a hostage, I reckon, but that won't save them. I'll run them down. And you'd better tell me right now if you know anything about what's going on, Della.'

'How should I know anything?' she countered.

'I need to know where you stand. If you know anything about Cullen's presence in town then you better get it off your chest right now.'

'How many times do I have to say it?' I told you the truth. I know I get all types in the saloon, but I draw the line at known outlaws.'

'Someone is trying to make a monkey outa me. And they took Joey!'

'They won't harm him,' Della said soothingly.

'Are you sure of that? Did Cullen tell you so when he was in here earlier?'

Della grimaced. She could see that nothing she said would improve the situation. 'I'm sorry about Joey,' she said. 'There's nothing more I can say. You'd better leave, Jim, before we say things that may ruin our friendship.'

Donovan stared into her set face, his eyes ugly with conflicting emotions. Then he turned on his heel and walked out of the office. He marched through the saloon to the batwings, stamped along the sidewalk and paused at the door of the freight office. A light was showing in the big front window and he peered inside; Abe Williams was seated at his desk. He entered noisily, and Williams sprang to his feet.

'Did you catch Cullen?' Williams demanded.

'Della said you were mistaken. So what's going on, Abe? Why did you lie to me?'

'I'm not a liar.' Anger rasped in Williams' voice. 'I told you what I saw, like any good citizen would.'

'Someone is lying,' Donovan countered.

'Well it ain't me!' Williams smacked his right fist into the palm of his left hand. Anger sparkled in his eyes. 'I know what I saw, and I recognized Cullen without hesitation. I've told you I saw him, and what you do about it is your business.'

'I'm assuming Cullen busted Elroy Johnson out of the jail after you said you saw him. And he took my brother Joey along with him. I need to find Joey pretty damn quick before something bad happens to him. So you'd better be telling me the truth, Williams, because if I find out you are fooling me I won't be responsible for my actions.'

'I'll swear on a stack of Bibles that I told you the truth,' Williams said aggressively. 'Now you better get outa here before I lose my temper. I don't like being called a liar, Donovan.'

Donovan turned on his heel and departed. He was seething inwardly as he walked along the street, consumed by a feeling of helplessness. He knew there was nothing he could do until daylight, when he could look for tracks and hunt down the horses that had stood behind the jail. But hours of waiting and fearing the worst stood between him and the moment he could act, and his impatience and frustration were overwhelming. He went back to the jail, found the office locked and cursed under his breath. He had expected the sheriff to remain on hand in this present emergency, but when he unlocked the door he found a note on the desk, written in Turner's hand, indicating that the sheriff had gone home to his bed.

He entered the cell block and stared at Watson, stretched out on the bunk, asleep and snoring, his nose swollen, his battered face smeared with blood. Donovan drew his pistol and banged on the bars of the door. Watson jerked, opened his eyes and gazed implacably at Donovan.

'You'd better start coming up with some right answers,' Donovan grated. 'I'm through pussy-footing around. Tell me what was going on tonight and you might live to see the sun come up in the morning, but hold out on me and you'll suffer for it. So start giving out, mister.'

'I've told you; you've got the wrong man.'

'I know you ride with Stomp Cullen, so tell me about Sam Rouse.

'Rouse? What about him? Has he been arrested?'

'It's better than that.' Donovan smiled grimly. 'I killed him this morning.'

'That's nothing to me. I don't know anyone named Rouse.'

'He's known to ride with Cullen, and so are you.'

Donovan went into the front office, picked up Watson's Wanted dodger, and took it back into the cell block. He held out the yellowed paper and waved it to attract Watson's attention.

'Here's a picture of your ugly mug,' he declared. 'Look at it and then deny it's you. Quit stalling or I'll beat the hell outa you. My kid brother has been dragged into this, and he comes first with me.'

'You're wasting your breath,' Watson responded. 'That picture don't prove a thing. It could be any one of a dozen other guys. Lemme get some sleep now. You've had your fun.'

Donovan seethed, but turned away from the cell and went back into the front office. He sat at the desk and riffled through the wanted dodgers again, picking out other members of the Cullen gang – men like Shap Kelly, Pete Coe, Hank Fargus and Dick Leggett – and wondered what they were planning. Whatever they were up to, it could only mean trouble for Lodestone.

He put his feet up on the desk, eased his Stetson over his eyes and tried to sleep, impatient for the morning to arrive. He was bone weary but his brain was whirling and he was gripped by worry. His thoughts were mainly for his brother. Joey wouldn't understand what was happening to him, and, with a man like Elroy Johnson in his company, anything could happen. . . .

At that moment Joey was trotting along on a horse with Elroy Johnson at his side. Two strangers were riding behind them – the men who had busted Johnson out of jail. Joey was glad to be out of his cell, and did not mind riding with Johnson, for there was something in the badman's manner that appealed to him. He looked on Johnson as a friend. Johnson was suffering pain from his shoulder wound, and found the ride tough going. He swayed in his saddle whenever the horse broke its stride, and groaned in agony at the incessant jolting he had to endure. But he was free, and he passed the time planning what he would do to Jim Donovan when they met again.

'Where are we going, Elroy?' Joey demanded for the tenth time, his shrill tone cutting through Johnson's agony.

'Look, I ain't feeling so good with this shoulder so gimme a break and shut your mouth for a spell,' grated Johnson through clenched teeth. 'This ain't no Sunday school outing. We're heading for your brother's horse ranch, and we're gonna wait there until he shows up looking for you.'

'What are you gonna do when Jim comes? You don't wanta get on the wrong side of my brother. He ain't pleased with you, Elroy, and might whale the tar outa you for busting the jail.'

'I didn't bust out,' Johnson rasped irritably. 'Cullen, back there, turned me loose. So let it rest, can't you? Let me concentrate on what I've gotta do.'

'Hey, Joey, why don't you do like Johnson says, huh?' Cullen, big, powerful and heavy-set, came up on Joey's left. 'Button your lip, kid. Heck, you talk nineteen to the dozen! Give us all a break and stop beating our ears with your cackle. You're going to your hoss ranch, and you'll be staying there with Johnson till your brother shows up.'

Joey glanced sideways at Cullen. He did not like the outlaw's manner or anything about him. He could sense the callousness in the big stranger; aware that here was a man he could not play his usual youthful tricks on. He fell silent, and they rode on through the night until Cullen called a halt.

'You'll be OK now, Johnson,' Cullen said. 'Leggett and me will go on to my sister's ranch. You stay where you're going until you're able to move around easy, and you know what to do if Donovan shows up looking for his brother. I'll send Leggett to see you every now and then. Don't get into any more trouble, and if you reckon you can't handle Donovan then I'll send Pete Coe to help you. An extra gun might make all the difference.'

'Yeah, sure, Cullen' Johnson rasped. 'But you can leave it to me. I've waited a long time to get Jim Donovan in my sights. I'll nail him when he shows up.'

'You better get rid of the kid when you've done for his brother,' Cullen observed, and galloped off into the night, followed by Leggett.

Joey waited until the two riders had vanished into the shadows before he spoke. 'I don't like them, Elroy. They talk like they want Jim dead. You're not gonna shoot my brother, are you? He's all I got.'

'Where'd you get that idea from, Joey? Jim and me are long-time friends. There's no trouble between us. Jim had to put me in jail because I broke the law once. I respect him for what he stands for. He told me to bring you out here to your place because he's worried something bad might happen to you back in Lodestone. That Preston feller's got the idea that you killed Martha and robbed the store, and he's like to come after you with a gun. That's why Jim asked me to bring you out here where you'll be safe.'

'So Jim knows you're out of our jail?' Joey mused.

'He sent Cullen along to bust me out,' Johnson said. 'Being a deputy, he couldn't do it himself so he sent some friends of mine to handle it.'

Joey was satisfied, and settled down to the ride. Dawn was breaking when Johnson reined up on a rise and gazed at the lonely horse ranch in the middle distance that was the Donovan family home. A curl of smoke licked up from the stone chimney, and there were two horses in the corral set behind the small ranch house.

'Jim is here already,' Joey said excitedly. 'It looks like he's cooking breakfast for us. Come on, let's get down there and see him.'

'They'll be my friends here,' Johnson said. 'Don't give either of them any lip or you'll be the worse for it. Come on. I wanta hit the sack.'

As they rode down into the yard a man carrying a rifle stepped out from the front corner of the house and confronted them.

'It's about time you showed up, Johnson,' he greeted. He was tall and heavy, his face fleshy. A battered black Stetson was pulled down low over his snake-like brown eyes. The butt of a .45 pistol nestled in the holster of the cartridge belt buckled around his ample waist. His expression changed when he saw Johnson's bandaged shoulder. 'Say, what happened to you, Elroy? Did you try for Jim Donovan?'

'I bumped into Donovan in town,' Johnson snarled. 'What's it to you, Mack?

'And you got the worst of it, huh? So who's the kid?'

'Joey Donovan. We're gonna wait for his big brother to come on out.'

'You better get down before you fall off that horse. Harper is inside, doing breakfast. Go right in and I'll take care of your horses.'

Johnson slid out of the saddle and staggered to the front door, motioning for Joey to follow. They entered the house, and a short, fat man straightened from the stove. The appetizing smell of frying bacon made Joey realize just how hungry he was.

'So you finally got here,' Harper commented. 'Who's your friend?' An easy smile showed on his lips but his narrowed eyes were like chips of frozen blue sky. 'Are you hungry, kid?'

'Starving,' Joey replied. 'That smells real good.'

'Pull up a chair, then. It's about ready.' Harper poured boiling water into a coffee pot and added a handful of coffee.

Johnson explained the situation when they were seated around the table. Harper grinned at Joey.

'This is Jim's ranch.' Joey said. 'Are you gonna work for him?'

'Yeah, that's about right.' Harper grinned, and Joey warmed to him. 'You just take it easy around here and we'll all wait for your brother to show up.' He went to the door, jerked it open, and called to the guard. 'It's ready, Mack. Come and get it.'

Mack Kett came in. He glared at Joey as he sat down opposite.

'You got a job someplace?' he demanded, and Joey shook his head.

'The folks in Lodestone won't give me a chance,' he said. 'They think I'm too much of a kid.'

'Why is that?' Harper asked. 'You look big enough to handle anything they got in town.'

'Leave him alone,' Johnson said irritably. 'He's short on savvy. The way I heard it, he fell down that well out in the yard, banged his head, and ain't been right since. So just keep an eye on him. Cullen said we should hold him here because he'll bring Jim Donovan nosing around looking for him, and then we'll be able to nail him. Soon as Donovan is dead Cullen will move into Lodestone to handle the bank. Just keep an eye on Joey.'

'Can you play poker, Joey?' Harper asked.

'Have you got any dough to play with?' Kett added with a grin.

Johnson moaned and groaned his way through

the meal and then lurched to his feet.

'I'm gonna hit the sack in the back room,' he said. 'You two keep a close eye on things, and don't let Joey run wild. Give me a call if anyone shows up. I don't wanta be caught napping.'

He went into the back room. Kett went outside to resume his guard duty, and Joey helped Harper clean up after the meal. When he had finished his chores, Joey went outside to look around. Kett emerged from around the front corner of the house.

'You stay inside, kid,' he said. 'No one knows we're here, and we wanta keep it that way.'

'I used to live here,' Joey protested. 'My pa ran horses here till he died.'

'Is that a fact?' Kett gazed at him. 'So you banged your head and screwed up your brains, huh? Did you have any schooling?'

'Not after I fell down the well.'

'So what do you do with yourself every day?'

'I find odd jobs here and there.'

'OK, now get back inside the house and stay put.'

'I wanta look around,' Joey protested.

Kett grasped Joey's shoulder, opened the door and thrust him into the house. Joey fell against the table and dropped to the floor, surprised and hurt by the rough treatment. He got up, rubbing a bruised elbow, and went to the window to peer out at Kett, who walked out of sight around the house.

Joey rapidly reassessed his opinion of these men. Now he didn't like them. He thought over what had been said, and recalled that someone mentioned killing Jim when he showed up. Joey frowned, not liking that thought. These men were not friends of his brother, and maybe he should warn Jim that they were here waiting for him. He looked at Harper, now sitting at the table and reading an old newspaper. Joey went back to the door, opened it a crack and peered out. If he was going to warn Jim about these men then he would need a horse to get back to town.

There was no sign of Kett outside, and Joey sneaked out of the house and made for the nearest corner. He looked down the side of the house to the rear, saw no sign of Kett, and ran swiftly to the rear corner. When he looked around the corner he saw Kett disappearing into the small barn. He studied the horses in the corral, and wondered if he could take one of them without being seen, for he had no doubts now about what would happen to him if these men caught him trying to escape.

He ran across the open space between the house and the barn and dropped flat on the ground just past the front corner of the barn. There were gaps in the sun-warped boards and he peered through a narrow aperture and studied the inside. The interior was gloomy, and excitement flared in his mind when he saw Kett sitting on a bale of straw, rolling a cigarette. Always ready to play a joke or a trick on some unsuspecting victim, Joey was fired up about escaping. He got to his feet and went to the rear of the barn, and then cut across to the corral, where four horses were penned. He picked up a bridle from the shed beside the corral, slid under the bottom rail, and approached the horse he had ridden when leaving town.

Accustomed as he was to handling animals, Joey slipped the bridle on the horse and led the animal to the entrance. He slid the poles back, jumped on the horse and urged it around the others until he was behind them. Then he shouted and waved an arm, driving the horses out of the corral and followed them closely as they galloped towards a nearby ridge. It was no hardship for him to ride bareback. He laughed aloud in sheer excitement, until a rifle cracked in the doorway of the barn and a bullet snarled in his left ear. He ducked, lay flat along the back of the horse, and kicked the animal into greater effort. More slugs crackled around him but he was untouched, and moments later he passed over the rise.

Excited but not sure of what to do next, he looked around for his bearings and then set off for town, following the horses he had freed. He wanted to see Jim, and he urged his mount on to greater effort. . . .

FIVE

Della slept badly that night, and arose before dawn to dress in riding gear: denim pants, white shirt, a short, faded blue tunic-type jacket, topped off with a flat-brimmed grey Stetson. She buckled a gun belt around her waist, checked the .38 pistol in the holster and left the hotel by the back door. Dawn was showing as just a grey streak in the east as she made her way to the livery barn for her horse. Minutes later she was mounted on her white mare and heading for her horse ranch, fifteen miles to the south-west.

Her unrest was caused by the knowledge that her brother, Stomp Cullen, was back in Lodestone. She had lied to Donovan about seeing the outlaw. Cullen was family, and she had told him to go out to her ranch and stay there out of sight until she was able to visit him. She had questioned him about his reasons for turning up like a bad penny, and had not believed him when he said his only wish was to see her. She suspected that he was planning to rob the local bank, and, if he succeeded then her nest egg of fifty thousand dollars in the bank safe would surely disappear without trace.

At first she had considered informing Donovan of her brother's visit, but Donovan had forestalled her by turning up and questioning her about Cullen, making her realize that shooting was inevitable if Donovan got on Cullen's trail. She didn't want anyone getting hurt in a showdown.

She rode at a fast clip through growing daylight, intent on buying off Cullen and restoring the even tenor of her life in Lodestone. She feared that Martha Preston's murder during the robbery at the store had been committed by Cullen or one of his men, and more of the same could be expected if Cullen was not bought off.

Two hours after sunup she rode into the ranch to find that Cullen had been and gone. Her ranch foreman, Hank Jessup, a big, powerful man, taciturn but intensely loyal to Della, was angry as he related how Cullen had threatened and tried to bully him but failed.

'So he's gone, has he?' Della demanded.

'He pulled out just after sunup. He said he had things to do.'

'Which way did he ride? He didn't pass me and I came straight from town.'

'He rode off in the opposite direction,' said Jessup sourly. 'But knowing what a sneaky cuss he is, I wouldn't be surprised if he didn't circle later and head somewhere else. He said to tell you that you wouldn't see him again. I got the feeling you didn't make him welcome in Lodestone. He reckoned there's no family feeling between you two now so he's cutting his losses.'

Della relaxed visibly as she considered. 'Throw my saddle on another horse, Hank. I'll return to town after I've had some breakfast and a rest. Give me a couple of hours, huh?'

'Sure thing. I'll tell Cookie to throw some grub together for you and bring it over. You won't be happy when you look in the house. Cullen went through the place before he pulled out. I heard him doing it.'

'Thanks, Hank. But it's no more than I would expect from my brother. I just hope he has gone for good, but I have my doubts. I didn't like the drift of his talk when I saw him in town last evening.'

She went into the house, and was angered by the sight of her possessions strewn around. Drawers had been pulled out and thrown on the floor; cupboard doors stood open, their contents dumped haphazardly. A thorough search had been made, and she paused in the doorway of her office in dismay at the sight of her ledgers and files lying around like so much waste paper. The big metal cash box was open on the desk, and when she checked it – for she kept a pile of ready cash on hand usually amounting to a thousand dollars – she found it was empty.

Her anger faded as she considered. If Cullen had

really gone for good then losing a thousand dollars to him would be well worth it. But she had her doubts. She had unwittingly mentioned her second ranch, off to the west, which she had recently purchased, and she wondered if Cullen had gone there to take whatever he could find.

Bill Denny, the cook, arrived with breakfast to find Della busily restoring orderliness to the office. She ate, and later, when starting the long ride back to town, she was filled with hope that she had seen the last of her callous brother. In any case, her attitude to him had hardened since last evening. They were really finished, and this time she meant it. However, when she was out of sight of the ranch she changed her mind and her direction and headed for the old Alpin place, her new acquisition, for she suspected that Cullen would head there next and she was determined to have a final showdown with him. . . .

Donovan was awake long before dawn, and left a note in the law office for Dan Turner, informing the sheriff that he planned to hunt down Johnson and locate Joey. The sun was barely above the skyline when he collected his horse from the livery barn about an hour after Della had left town. He rode along the rear of the buildings fronting the street, dismounted at the back of the jail and examined the horse tracks he had seen there. Four animals had stood for a while, and then moved off, leaving hoof prints in the thick dust. He stepped up into his saddle and set out to follow them.

The tracks led him south and west through rough country, and Donovan began to speculate when he realized he was riding towards his own ranch, which had stood vacant since he took on the job of deputy sheriff. When he became certain of his destination he pushed on at a faster clip to cover the ten miles. He was some two miles from the spread when he heard the sound of shots, and spurred his horse into a gallop, heading for a rise before him.

He dismounted just before reaching the skyline. There had been three shots and then an ominous silence. He dragged his rifle from its boot and bellied down as he reached the crest. When he glanced over the rise he saw a horse lying at the bottom of a slope, and a figure, which he recognized instantly as Joey, standing motionless and looking down at it. A rider was approaching his brother with a levelled rifle. The rider, a stranger, reined up beside Joey. Donovan ran back to his horse and swung into the saddle. He slid the rifle back into its boot, rode over the rise, and galloped towards the scene.

The rider was threatening Joey with the long gun. Joey turned his back on the man and started up the slope, until he saw Donovan bearing down on him. The rider heard the pounding hoofs and looked up. He lifted his rifle and Donovan pulled his pistol and began shooting.

Joey dropped flat in his tracks when Donovan's bullet crackled over his head. The slug struck the rider in the right side and he dropped his rifle. When he reached for his holstered pistol, Donovan fired again, and the slug took the man in the centre of the chest. He fell sideways out of the saddle, thumped on the hard ground and remained motionless. Joey sprang up and did a war dance, whooping in excitement, waving his arms and stamping as he circled the fallen man. His voice echoed and re-echoed as he gave vent to his relief.

Donovan checked his surroundings as he approached his brother. He stepped down from his saddle and pushed Joey away before dropping to one knee beside the downed rider. The man was dead; blood had spread in a crimson stain across his chest.

'So what happened, Joey?' Donovan demanded.

Joey was quivering with excitement. 'You got him dead centre, Jim!' he exclaimed. 'I thought he was gonna kill me, and I didn't do nothing to him. I was riding back to town on that horse and he shot it from under me.'

'Settle down,' Donovan encouraged. 'Tell it from the beginning. I left you in a cell last night, so how come you're out here with a dead horse? What happened?'

'It was Elroy Johnson let me out of the cell.' Joey creased his forehead as he recalled the incidents of the past hours. 'Two men busted Johnson outa your jail, Jim.'

'What two men?'

'One of them was called Cullen. I remember that

name real good because I didn't like him. He told Johnson to ride to our place and wait there for you to show up and then kill you. Two other men were waiting at our ranch when we rode in; living in the house. I sneaked away from them after breakfast. I took one of the horses and drove the other three outa the corral when I left. Johnson and the other two ain't got horses. I left them afoot. Jim. Did I do right?'

'You did real good, Joey. Where did Cullen go when he left you?'

'He talked about riding to a horse ranch. That could only be Della's place, I reckon.'

'Then this guy turned up and shot your horse,' Donovan prompted. 'Who is he?'

'I don't know. Perhaps Johnson sent him after me because I chased off their horses.'

'And Johnson is waiting at our place for me to ride in so he can shoot me,' Donovan mused.

'He's planning it that way, but he couldn't best you in a month of Sundays.' Joey laughed and started his war dance again. Donovan shouted at him and he stood still.

Donovan glanced around. The skyline was clear. 'I'll tell you what I want you to do, Joey. Get up on that horse and ride back to town. Go straight to the law office, see Sheriff Turner, and tell him to put you back in a cell until I show up. You got that?'

'Sure thing, Jim. I'll do like you say.'

'Then get moving.'

'What are you gonna do?'

'Never mind what I'm gonna do. When I get back to town I wanta see you safe and sound in a cell.'

'Suppose Cullen comes after me again? I'd be a lot safer with you, and I wanta see the action if you're gonna shoot Johnson.'

'I've told you what to do so get up on that horse and hightail it to town.' Donovan pushed Joey towards the horse and Joey jumped up into the saddle.

'Gimme the rifle in case anyone tries to stop me, Jim,' Joey said.

'You know what I've told you about guns. You don't need one. Go on, get outa here. I'll be back in town before long.'

Joey pulled a face and set his heels into the flanks of the horse. The animal started forward and Joey rode up the slope and disappeared over the rise. Donovan swung into his saddle, rode to the top of the rise and sat his mount to watch Joey's progress towards the town until the boy was lost to sight. Then he turned and set off at a fast run for the horse ranch, where he expected to find Johnson and his companions without horses and at a big disadvantage.

At dawn that morning, out at Della Jordan's horse ranch, Stomp Cullen was sitting in the kitchen eating breakfast. One by one his gang members showed up to join him, and he studied them critically as they sat around the table. They were a good bunch, all callous killers well suited to the crimes Cullen planned and carried out. They rode far and wide through Colorado and neighbouring territories, robbing and murdering for their evil gains, and Cullen was cunning enough to evade the inevitable searches made for them.

'We're riding into Lodestone today,' Cullen announced as he pushed back his chair. He took a sack of Bull Durham from a pocket and rolled a cigarette. 'Eat your grub quick because I aim to ride out in fifteen minutes. Don't steal anything from this place. I'll go through it before we leave.'

'I wish I had a sister who owned a saloon,' observed Dick Leggett. He was tall and lean, sharp-featured, with small, crafty eyes. He wore his holstered six-shooter on his left thigh, and carried a Bowie knife in a sheath behind his back. Black stubble concealed his jawline, which was grown mainly to hide most of the tell-tale knife scar that adorned his left cheek from the corner of his mouth to his eyebrow.

'Be ready to ride when I call you,' Cullen directed. 'I'm wondering what happened to Rouse. I sent him into Lodestone early to watch the bank and then meet me back of the Golden Slipper last evening, but he didn't show up.'

'I reckon he went to the saloon and got himself a bellyful of likker,' said Pete Coe. 'You picked the wrong man to handle a chore like that.'

'I'll make him wish he'd never been born if he did that,' Cullen promised.

'Della's foreman thinks he's real tough,' Shap Kelly declared. His dark eyes gleamed as he looked at Cullen, hoping the gang boss would tell him to take care of the man. He was under-sized, no more than five feet in his boots, and carried a chip on his shoulder about his lack of height. 'Maybe we should put him down before he talks about us coming here.'

'Do nothing to queer our pitch,' Cullen rasped. 'We might wanta come back here to hide out if things go wrong in Lodestone. Now quit yapping and get moving. I wanta be riding.'

Cullen went around his sister's home, almost wrecking the office looking for spare cash and raided the cash box before he was ready to leave. When he rode out at the head of his gang he was well pleased with the situation. He had left his mark for Della to take note that he didn't think blood was thicker than water. . . .

Donovan reined in just below the crest of the rise that overlooked his ranch. The sun was high overhead. He left his horse in cover and took his rifle to a spot where he could look down on the little cluster of buildings where he had been born. His eyes glinted when he spotted a man seated on a chair just outside the door of the house, and smiled when he recognized Elroy Johnson, sunning himself as if he owned the place. Johnson looked as if he had fallen asleep. His head was back, his mouth agape.

The place looked otherwise deserted, Donovan thought, and he wondered where the other two men Joey had mentioned had gone; probably trying to round up their scattered horses. Joey had excelled himself by turning the animals loose. He had tied Johnson down to this spot, and Donovan prepared to move in and arrest the wounded badman.

Donovan remounted and set out to circle the ranch buildings, wanting to sneak in from the rear and catch Johnson napping. He gained the rear of the barn and left his horse standing tied to a post. He was sneaking forward to the back of the house when he heard the sudden rapid tattoo of several horses approaching the yard out front. He dropped into cover and drew his pistol.

He crouched in the shadow of the house and waited, listening to harsh voices in the yard and wondering who had arrived. He estimated half a dozen riders had turned up, and wondered if Sheriff Turner had formed a posse, a theory which he quickly discounted. Johnson had evidently been caught napping, for there were no sounds of resistance, and then he heard Johnson talking in a friendly tone to whoever had showed up.

Donovan sneaked down the far side of the house and gained the front corner. He dropped flat on his stomach, removed his Stetson and edged forward until he could peer around the corner. There were five riders sitting their horses in front of Johnson; he recognized Stomp Cullen immediately. The gang boss was leaning forward, both hands resting on his saddle-horn, his face expressionless; hard gaze boring into Johnson.

'So you fouled up again, Johnson,' Cullen was saying. 'You ain't done too well since you've been back. We busted you outa prison and you ain't got anything right. Hell. I've got a good mind to take you back to Lodestone and put you back behind bars. You couldn't even handle a halfwit kid who's still wet behind the ears, and you reckoned you could take Jim Donovan. Hell, you couldn't do that even in your dreams. And you got yourself shot up so you can't do anything except sit here sunning yourself. I paid good dough to spring you loose from the big pen, and you turned out to be a liability. I reckon you got nothing going for you but a big mouth.'

'It was just bad luck,' Johnson protested. 'It could have happened to anyone. I tell you I can handle Donovan, and he'll being showing up any time now. We baited a trap and he'll sure come around.'

'But you don't have the kid any more. He's gone to hunt up his big brother and explain what he's done, and Jim Donovan will come here, all right, looking for blood – your blood.'

'He'll get a slug between the eyes when I see him,' Johnson promised. Donovan wondered at his luck, but was realistic enough to accept that he could not tackle odds of six to one. His pulses quickened as he reached an immediate decision. He eased back from the corner and crawled away several yards before getting to his feet and heading for his horse. He knew Johnson would not be moving far from where he was sitting, and could be picked up later, so when Cullen rode out with his gang, Donovan intended being on the outlaws' trail.

He was crossing the open space between the house and the barn on his way to his horse when a voice called to him. He swung in the direction the voice came from and saw two riders coming towards him from beyond the corral. When he started running to the cover of the barn both men pulled their pistols and cut loose at him, tearing the silence to shreds with their gun clamour and hurling harsh echoes to the horizon.

Donovan snapped off a couple of shots in their direction and they split, riding in opposite directions. He lunged into the barn and ran straight through to the back, where his horse was tethered outside. One of the riders came into the barn behind him, shooting rapidly, while the other rode along the outside to cover the rear. Donovan spun and dropped to one knee. The rider in the doorway hauled his mount back on its haunches and dived from the saddle. Donovan got him with a single shot as the man hit the ground on his right shoulder. His gun went flying and he rolled on to his back and remained motionless.

The sound of rapid hoofs outside the barn warned Donovan what he could expect if he went for his horse. He paused just inside the back door and peered around the door post. A slug clipped the edge of the door with a deadly thud. Donovan dropped flat in a forward dive and lifted his gun to cover the rider, who had halted outside, gun uplifted ready for a shot. Donovan fired instantly. Echoes reverberated inside the barn and gunsmoke flared. The rider twisted in his saddle and went over backward, dropping his gun and following it swiftly to the sun-baked ground.

Donovan got to his feet and ran to his horse. He sprang into the saddle, jerked the reins free from the post, and hit a gallop in a few strides, swinging away from the barn but keeping it between him and the house. He fully expected the gang to come after him when they heard the shooting, and he rode with his chin on his left shoulder, watching his back. He had covered fifty yards before he saw two riders appear at a front corner of the house. The next instant two more riders emerged through the back doorway of the barn.

Gunfire erupted and slugs snarled around Donovan. He did not return fire but concentrated on riding, and when he saw two of the riders follow him in pursuit he faced front and checked his surroundings. He had been born on this ranch and knew the immediate range intimately. He headed north, to broken ground and timber, watching his pursuers intently. They stopped shooting at him and concentrated on riding him down. Donovan headed for the nearest rise.

He hammered up a rock-strewn slope, passed over the crest and, when he was out of sight of his pursuers, dismounted and jerked his Winchester from its boot. He threw himself down on the hard ground and eased forward until he could cover the slope. The two riders had separated and were riding right and left to get out of range. When they started up the slope he fired two shots at the right-hand rider. The horse went down. Donovan got up and ran to his own horse.

If he could shorten the odds against him he knew he had a good chance of catching Cullen unawares. The gang boss had evidently remained at the ranch, and without big odds against him, Donovan was certain he could wipe out the gang. He swung slightly to reach a gorge, and when he looked back he saw that a single rider was following.

He halted, stepped down from his saddle and drew his pistol. The rider halted immediately, then swung his horse and began to ride back to the ranch. Donovan remounted and continued, angling west, making for a ravine that cut into the ridge ahead. He permitted his horse to pick its way through the inclining cleft, and when he emerged at the top he turned left along the skyline and continued until he reached a spot from where he could look down on his ranch buildings.

There were no signs of life on the ranch, and no horses around. The house looked deserted, the front door closed. Donovan sat his horse and gazed around subjecting the whole area to a close scrutiny. He followed the line of the trail that led to Lodestone, and spotted tell-tale signs of drifting dust in the air. He nodded as he considered that several horses had gone onwards, making for town, and he continued, using a short cut that only a man familiar with the area would know.

The going was easier along the short cut, and he pushed his horse relentlessly. Great peaks raised their heads around him in the distance, with foothills closer to hand. But Donovan had no eyes for the grandeur of the rugged scene. He kept the main trail in sight, and eventually spotted a group of four riders heading for Lodestone. He considered distances, and realized that he could not make the town before Cullen and the gang. He continued until his trail converged on the main trail and petered out, and then dropped back to conceal his presence.

He recognized Johnson riding with Cullen, and that pleased him. When the gang neared the outskirts of Lodestone, Cullen suddenly left the trail and made for the rear of the buildings to the right-hand side. Donovan went to the left and rode into an alley almost opposite the law office. He left his horse with its reins tied to a post in the cover of the alley and walked across the street to the jail, moving casually, his right hand close to the butt of his holstered pistol. He was tired, but fired up and hopeful of catching Cullen unawares.

The law office door was locked, and he wondered what the sheriff was doing as he unlocked it. There was a prickling sensation between his shoulder blades. The Cullen gang was in town, and he sensed that they were about to rob the bank. The law office was deserted and he went through to the cells. Relief speared through him when he saw Joey sitting disconsolately on a bunk in one of the cells and Noll Watson, apparently asleep, in another.

Joey sprang off the bunk when he saw Donovan.

'Did you kill Johnson?' the youngster demanded.

'Not yet. What happened here when you rode in? Where's the sheriff?'

'He said he had to go home. He ain't feeling so good.'

'That figures!' Donovan shook his head. 'OK. You sit tight in here. I've got some chores to handle. I'll be back in time to take you to the diner, if you behave yourself. Have you got that?'

'Sure thing.' Joey grinned. 'There ain't much I can do in here, is there?'

'That's a relief. I'll be back later.'

Donovan went to the back door and unbolted it. He peered out, and then closed the door silently, for Johnson and one of Cullen's gang were sitting their mounts just outside. Donovan drew his gun. He eased the door open a fraction to take another look, and frowned when he saw Cullen and another of the gang in the distance, riding away from the town. He sighed in annoyance, for he was still at a disadvantage. But he was intent on putting Johnson back behind bars. He checked his pistol, prepared for action the instant Cullen was out of earshot.

SIX

Donovan held the back door of the jail open a couple of inches and watched Johnson and his outlaw companion through the narrow crack. The two men were standing about ten yards out, talking with their heads together until the outlaw suddenly took the reins of Johnson's horse and led both animals away. Johnson turned into the alley beside the jail. Donovan closed the door until he heard Johnson's footsteps pass by, and then peered out and watched him leave the alley to head across the street. He bolted the door and ran through to the front office to look out the window. Johnson was entering Doc Hardy's office.

Joey called Donovan, and he returned to the cells.

'What is it, Joey? I'm busy right now. I'm gonna pick up Johnson.'

'Will you bring him back here?' Joey asked. 'I like talking to Elroy.'

'He won't wanta talk to you after turning those

horses loose out at the ranch,' Donovan replied. 'Now settle down.'

He checked his pistol again as he went to the street door. The street was deserted, and he crossed it, heading for the doctor's office. He glanced around, looking for trouble. In the back of his mind was the thought that Cullen was riding away from town. He reached the doctor's house and entered. The office was on the left, the door closed. Donovan drew his pistol and grasped the handle. He threw open the door, levelled his gun, and strode in.

Johnson was seated on a couch, his shirt off. Doc Hardy was taking the bandage off Johnson's injured shoulder. Hardy looked up, a protest on his lips. Johnson reached for the gun in his holster. Donovan stepped forward a couple of swift paces and slammed the muzzle of his pistol against Johnson's injured shoulder. Johnson screeched, sprang up out of the chair and then fell to the floor, yelling in agony.

'Sorry to interrupt, Doc.' Donovan picked up Johnson's discarded gun. 'I need to put him back where he belongs.' He stuck the pistol in the waistband of his pants. 'Come on, Elroy, your cell is waiting.'

When Elroy didn't move, Donovan reached down, grasped him by the scruff of the neck, and hauled him upright.

'Let me bandage his shoulder before you leave,' Doc Hardy said.

'Sorry.' Donovan shook his head. 'I don't have the

time. I've got things to do that won't wait. Come across to the jail later. Johnson will be waiting.'

He thrust Johnson to the door and they departed. Donovan was alert as they went on to the law office. Johnson was holding his right hand against his wounded shoulder and blood was trickling between his fingers. He had lost all interest in escaping. In the office, Donovan paused to lock the street door, and then put Johnson in a cell, well away from Joey, on the far side of Noll Watson.

'Joey, you sit quiet until I get back,' Donovan warned.

He departed and went along the street to the saloon. He wanted the outlaw who had remained with Johnson, and guessed that the Golden Slipper was the first place the man would visit. He pushed through the batwings, his cold gaze flitting around the long room, and, although there were some half dozen men present, the outlaw was not one of them. He went to the bar and Hatton came to confront him.

'What'll be, Jim?'

'Not right now, thanks. I'm looking for a tall, lean guy wearing a red shirt. He rode into town about fifteen minutes ago so he's a Johnnie-come-lately.'

'No one like that has come in,' Hatton replied.

Donovan grimaced. 'OK, so is Della around?'

'I ain't set eyes on her.' Hatton shook his head.

'Have you any idea where she's gone?'

'Out to her ranch, I guess. She did mention she's

got some trouble out there.'

'OK, I'll check again later.'

Donovan departed, paused on the sidewalk to look around, and was just in time to see a man wearing a red shirt entering the freight line office along the street. He recognized the outlaw instantly, and went back along the sidewalk. But when he reached the door of the freight line office he stopped to consider. Why was an outlaw visiting Abe Williams? He recalled that Williams had reported seeing Cullen entering the rear of the saloon the previous evening. So what was going on? He began to think of Della's attitude when he had confronted her with the news that Cullen was seen entering her place. She had not reacted as he expected. There had been nothing overtly wrong in her manner, but he had sensed a strangeness about her that gave him the impression she had lied to him.

He sighed and drew his pistol. Whatever was going on, he could not let a known outlaw wander around town unchallenged. He went into the office, found himself in a short passage, which had several doors opening off it and paused outside the first door on the left, which he knew was the main office. He heard the murmur of voices coming from inside. Drawing a deep breath, he released it slowly before thrusting open the door and entering.

The outlaw, seated on a chair in front of a big, paper-strewn desk, sprang to his feet and reached for his gun. Donovan covered him with his pistol, and the outlaw halted his movement and held his hands clear of his waist. His dark eyes were glinting, his heavy face stained with shock.

Abe Williams, seated behind the desk, sprang to his feet, startled by Donovan's sudden appearance.

'What in hell is going on?' he demanded hoarsely. 'What are you up to, Donovan?'

'What's going on in here?' Donovan countered.

'This man came here looking for a job and I'm about to interview him for a vacancy,' Williams rasped. 'I'm always short of good wagon drivers. Why did you come busting in here like a wild bull? You're carrying your law dealing too far.'

Donovan, watching the outlaw intently, said: 'Sit down, Williams, and keep your mouth shut. I'll do the talking. You, mister, get rid of your gun belt right now or you'll never need another job.'

The outlaw unbuckled the belt and let it drop to the floor. 'I don't know who you think I am, Deputy,' he said, 'but you've got the wrong man. I ain't done nothing against the law.'

'What's your name?' Donovan demanded.

'Charlie Miller.'

'I've seen your face on a wanted dodger in the office,' Donovan continued, 'and Charlie Miller ain't the name the law knows you by. So let's take a walk along the street, read that dodger and get your real name.'

'You're making a big mistake,' Williams cut in.

'I told you to keep your mouth shut,' Donovan

warned. 'I'll come back to you later and we'll talk. OK, "Miller," if that's your name now, get moving. Out to the street and turn left. You'll know the law office when you get to it – there's a board above the door with SHERIFF on it.'

Miller shrugged and came forward. Donovan moved aside, staying out of arm's reach. They left the office and Miller turned left. Donovan stayed three paces behind as they went on to the law office. A voice hailed Donovan as he reached into his pocket for the key to the office and he glanced round to see the sheriff hurrying towards him.

'Who have you got there, Jim?' Turner demanded.

'He's Miller, so he says, but there's a dodger on him inside with a different name on it.'

'He looks like Shap Kelly,' Turner mused. 'I know his face. How'd you pick him up?'

'Let's put him behind bars before we talk,' Donovan retorted.

Turner nodded, produced his key and unlocked the door. They entered. Miller was locked in a cell. The sheriff grinned when he saw Johnson back behind bars. Donovan went through the wanted posters, and came up with Miller's face, and the name Shap Kelly.

'Told you I knew him,' Turner said. 'So what's been going on, Jim?'

Donovan recounted his activities of the day.

'Yeah,' Turner said, 'Joey came into the office when he got back this morning, and told me some of it. So you found Johnson out at your place.'

'Yeah, and I had a run-in there with Cullen and his gang. I nailed a couple of them. Then I picked up Kelly in Abe Williams' office. Williams was gonna give him a job. Dan, while I think of it, we're gonna have to get a couple of men in here to take care of the place while I'm doing my job. Johnson was busted out last night with no trouble at all. This place has got to be guarded night and day while we've got prisoners behind bars.'

'I agree,' Turner nodded. 'I'll get the part-time jailers in to handle the chore. They're dependable. I'll go talk to them now. What are you gonna do?'

'I reckon I should ride out and check on Cullen. I've got a feeling he is gonna hit the bank in town before too long.'

'Or a silver shipment from one of the local mines,' Turner added. 'So Williams was thinking of hiring an outlaw as a driver, huh? Maybe I should chase that up and see if I can get something going.'

'Let Kelly sweat for a bit. Perhaps he didn't know Watson is an outlaw. Give him some rope and maybe he'll hang himself. Get some gun help in here and I'll follow Cullen's tracks and check him out.'

'Maybe you should take a posse along.'

'Not yet. Let's try and get some idea of what's going on before we commit ourselves.'

'I'll leave it to you, Jim.' Turner shook his head ruefully. 'I ain't in a fit condition to sit a horse right now. I'll have to take it easy for a spell longer.'

Donovan left the office and fetched his horse from where he had left it. He rode along the alley beside the jail and set off in the direction he had seen Cullen ride. His keen gaze noted the tracks left by the two outlaws, and he pushed along fast, thinking that Cullen would not stray far from town if he was making plans to rob the bank. He had travelled some three miles when he spotted two riders ahead, toiling up a long, rocky slope, following a game trail. A frown touched his face when he realized that the trail Cullen was following led to the old Alpin ranch, which had stood derelict ever since Alpin had died three years before.

Donovan dropped back and stayed in cover, following the riders. If he could ensure that Cullen was hiding out at Alpin's place he could ride back to town for a posse. . . .

Della took a couple of short cuts to get to her new ranch. She had no stock there, but the town carpenter and a hired man were doing up the place to make it habitable. Two hours later she was on a high rocky point looking down into a basin formed by a circle of grey hills. In the basin stood the old Alpin place – a dilapidated, two-storey house, sundry sheds, a barn and a large corral. The basin was grass-covered, and a narrow stream meandered through it from north to south, filling a large creek to the right of the ranch house.

She halted for some minutes, admiring the scenery

and relishing the solitude. She could see the two men she employed; one on the roof of the house, making it weatherproof, and the other working on the front door, which was lying across two trestles in the yard. She noted that the corral had been fixed, and two horses were now penned in it. A number of the posts and rails of the corral had been down when she first looked over the little spread, but now it was as good as new, and she was pleased as she started down the slope to enter the basin.

She paused to let her mare drink from the creek, and looked around critically. She loved the silence and the wide, high sky, and thought she might retire here when her time came. The place was almost inaccessible, and that pleased her greatly.

As she rode up to the cabin the two men spotted her and stopped working. Frank Billings was the carpenter, and Rafe Carter an odd-job man who helped Billings around town.

'Howdy, Della?' Billings greeted, straightening from working on the door. He was middle-aged; hair greying, face wrinkled. His brown eyes twinkled as he studied her face. 'I was saying to Rafe earlier it was about time we saw you again.'

'You haven't wasted much time,' Della replied. 'I'm amazed by what you've done.'

'Wait till you get a look inside.' Billings was elated. He took great pride in his work. 'We've pulled out all the stops to get the job done. I hope you'll like it.'

'I'm sure I shall, Frank. You're a real craftsman.

Shall we take a look?'

He grinned and hurried forward to lead her inside, eager to show her around. Della paused and lifted a hand to Rafe Carter, perched on the roof, a much younger man, before following Billings. She was impressed by the interior when she looked in through the doorway. A table and four chairs, newly made, occupied the centre of the big room. She sat down on one of the chairs and rested her elbows on the table as she looked around. New cupboards were fixed to the walls around the kitchen area and there was a wardrobe in a corner next to the bed. There was a new wooden floor underfoot, and she arose to dance a few steps to test the solid boards.

'It's beautiful,' she observed. 'You've excelled yourself, Frank. And you're almost finished. It's a perfect job. I bless the day I found you.'

'All in a day's work, Della,' he replied, pride ringing in his tone. 'It gives me great pleasure to do good work. I've left doing the floors in the bedrooms until last. When it's all done we'll put the bed up there in the best room.'

'I can hardly wait to see it completed,' she said. 'Have there been any callers this week?'

'Nary a soul. Are you expecting anyone?'

'I hope not.' She shook her head, thinking of her brother, and experienced a sinking feeling when she considered him coming in here, besmirching the place with his presence. 'I was out at my other ranch early this morning, and thought I'd call in here on my way back to town. But I don't want to take up any of your time, Frank. I know you're anxious to get the job done.'

'We're well ahead of ourselves. It'll all be finished before another week is out.'

He broke off as the crash of a shot dispelled the silence, and looked around quickly. Della was startled, and froze when she heard a heavy dragging sound overhead, as if Rafe Carter was sliding off the roof.

'It's Rafe!' Billings shouted. He ran to the doorway and went out front, halting abruptly as Carter fell off the roof and crashed down on to the door laid across the trestles, where he lay inertly with blood seeping from a bullet hole in his chest.

Della stood frozen in shock, a hand to her mouth. Then she heard harsh laughter outside, and the sound of approaching hoofs. She ran to the door, gasping when she saw Cullen, and another man who was holding a drawn pistol, now in the act of taking aim at the unarmed Billings.

Della hurried outside and stood between the carpenter and the outlaw.

'Hey, I didn't know you was here,' Cullen shouted.

Della moved to where Carter was lying on the door. He was dead, his face contorted by his violent end. She turned to face Cullen, who dismounted and came swaggering forward, grinning.

'We thought he was robbing the place,' Cullen said, his eyes cold and remote.

'He was working for me,' Della said furiously. 'You'd better turn around and ride right out again. You're not welcome here, or at any place I own. You were at my horse ranch this morning, and robbed me. I want that money back now, or I might just tell the local law about you.'

'You're pushing your luck, Della.' A menacing tone crept into Cullen's voice. 'So you're my sister! Well it don't give you the right to turn on me. Sure I took your dough. You won't miss it, and me and the gang need some eating money until we get back in business. I'm real sorry about your hired help.'

'I want you to leave right now,' Della said.

'No way. A couple of my men are missing, and we're gonna stick around here until they show up, so shut your mouth. What are you doing here anyway? Are you keeping track of me?'

'You're a cold-blooded killer with no respect for anyone or anything.' Della's face was pale. Her voice trembled. 'You didn't have to shoot Rafe. He was a good, honest worker; something you've never been. Ride out of here now. I never want to see you again. You're no longer my brother. No self-respecting person would want to know you. If you don't leave I shall make it my business to inform the law of your whereabouts.'

'Quit the cackle, Della.' Cullen grinned. 'I told you we're staying here for a few days. We'll leave when we're good and ready, and not before.'

'I'll ride back to Lodestone now,' she said, 'and tell

the sheriff about you. He'll bring a posse out here. What you do about that is up to you, but if you've got any sense you'll pull out.'

Cullen swung his right hand around and struck her in the face with his calloused palm. She cried out and fell to her knees, where she remained gazing at him with disbelief in her eyes.

'I told you to hold your noise,' he growled, 'so do like I tell you. Go inside the house and get some grub ready. You ain't going back to town until I say so. And if I hear any more about you talking to the law I'll make you wish you'd never been born. Go on, get up and get moving. I don't wanta have to repeat myself.'

Della got to her feet. Her cheek was bruised from the blow she had received. Cullen stepped in close to her and she thought he was going to hit her again, but he snatched the .38 out of the holster on her hip.

'Can you use a gun?' he demanded, and grinned when she nodded. 'Well you ain't gonna practise on me. Get some grub ready.' He pushed her towards the doorway and turned to the motionless Billings. 'You got a gun on you?' he demanded and, when Billings shook his head, said: 'You better get back to your work. Do you ride back to town when you've finished for the day?'

'No, we're staying here till the job is done.'

'Dig a hole out back for your pard.' Cullen turned to his watching man. 'Dick, give him a hand – you shot the guy.'

Della staggered as she entered the house. Her

mind seemed frozen in shock. She began preparing a meal, but the first seeds of resistance were already growing in her mind. It had taken the wanton murder of an innocent man to finally point her to her duty, and if it was the last thing she did, she would ensure that her brother paid for his crimes.

Donovan watched Cullen and his sidekick pass out of sight over the skyline. He rode nearer to top of the rise and left his horse on a wide ledge some twenty feet below the rim. He was familiar with the country, having visited the Alpin ranch several times when the old man had been alive. He took his rifle with him and entered the basin on foot, finding cover at a spot that gave him a clear view of the ranch down in the basin.

Immediately below Donovan, Cullen and Dick Leggett were negotiating the slope to the level ground of the basin. A movement over to the right of the ranch house caught his eye and he saw a white horse making its way past the shimmering creek to the house. The rider was a woman, and he guessed it was Della. There was a man working on the roof and another hammering nails into the front door, which was lying flat on two trestles in front of the doorway.

So what was Della doing out here? Donovan watched her progress while speculating on her presence. He guessed she had been to her horse ranch on the other side of his place, and knew of the short cuts she must have used to get here. He had heard a rumour that she'd bought Alpin's place, and nodded as he watched the scene below. Della entered the house with Billings, whom Donovan recognized, and, minutes later, Cullen and his associate reached the floor of the basin and started towards the house.

Donovan was thinking that Della's presence proved his suspicion that she was somehow involved with Cullen. He waited to see what would happen when the outlaws reached the house, and was shocked when Rafe Carter was shot and fell off the roof. He witnessed Della's appearance out front, and frowned when Cullen slapped her. Then the gang boss snatched Della's pistol and pushed her towards the house. Donovan lay in cover watching, thinking over the sequence of events. It didn't seem likely that Della and Cullen were on friendly terms.

Billings took a long-handled sod-buster around the side of the house and began to dig. He was accompanied by the tall outlaw who had shot Carter. Donovan judged the distance from his position to the house as being two hundred yards. He waited, aware that he could do nothing until he had the edge. Fighting single-handed against experienced gun hands meant the odds were not in his favour. He needed to discover what Cullen was planning to do, so he settled down to watch events. He checked his weapons, aware that action could explode without warning, and he had to be ready for anything.

Thirty minutes passed. Billings was making real progress with the hole he was digging. Donovan stiffened into full alertness when Billings and the tall outlaw fetched Carter's body from where it had fallen and toted it around to the grave. The body was thrown into the hole. The outlaw watched Billings as he refilled the hole. When several inches of earth covered Carter, the outlaw drew his pistol. Donovan jacked a cartridge into the breech of his rifle and lifted it into the aim. The outlaw said something to Billings, who straightened and began to protest. Donovan sensed that the unarmed man was about to be murdered and drew a bead on the tall outlaw. He allowed for the breeze that was blowing from west to east, restrained his breathing and fired when the blade of the foresight covered his target.

The crash of the shot echoed and re-echoed across the basin. Donovan merely opened his left eye and watched the outlaw, who was in the act of taking aim at Billings. Then the rifle bullet smacked into him, spinning him around. The pistol flew from his hand and he jack-knifed before falling heavily. Billings did not hear the sound of the shot until after the outlaw hit the ground. Then he looked around wildly, wondering where the bullet had come from.

Donovan reloaded and swung his aim to cover the front doorway of the house. Cullen stuck his head outside and then withdrew it quickly. Donovan cast a glance at Billings, and was relieved when he saw the carpenter snatch up the tall outlaw's discarded pistol and start running towards the back of the house.

Gun echoes grumbled and dwindled. Donovan was happy with the situation. Cullen remained in the house, and looked as if he meant to stay there. Donovan got to his feet and started down the slope into the basin. The odds were now in his favour. . . .

SEVEN

After Donovan had left town, Sheriff Turner went into the cell block to consider his prisoners. Johnson was trying to sleep, groaning frequently as pain throbbed through his wounded shoulder; Noll Watson sat on the end of his bunk, gazing at the floor and Shap Kelly was leaning against the door of his cell.

'Hey, Sheriff,' Johnson called. 'I need the doc to look at my shoulder. It's giving me hell. It's turning bad, I reckon.'

'I'll fetch Doc over when the jailer arrives,' Turner said. 'He'll be on duty soon.'

Turner returned to the front office, ignoring Johnson's grumbles, and sank down on the chair behind the desk, grimacing at the pain lancing through his body; his left forearm ached abominably and there were red hot needles of agony stabbing through his left shoulder. The bone in the big toe of his right foot felt as if it had been roasted in a camp-fire, and it hurt when he put weight on it.

He reached into the bottom right-hand drawer of the desk, took out a near-full bottle of whiskey and had a couple of long pulls. It was the only thing that helped deaden the pain. He sat waiting for the whiskey to take effect, and then took two more gulps for good measure. He was thinking seriously of retir-ing, but felt reluctant to take the momentous step.

The street door was jerked open and Art Walsh entered the office. Walsh, a one-time friend of Elroy Johnson and an ex-rustler who had never been caught, was an odd-job man around town and worked for the law whenever he was needed. He could turn his hand to anything; a cheerful, happy man with no responsibilities beyond a caring wife. He carried a paper packet containing food, and had a double-barrelled shotgun under his right arm. He put the packet on a corner of the desk and propped the shotgun against the wall beside it. He was tall and heavily built, and his blue eyes twinkled as he greeted the sheriff.

'Howdy, Dan,' he greeted.

'I'm glad you're on time, Art. I've got some ques-tions to ask around town so you'll be here alone for a spell. Don't take any chances. Keep the street door locked at all times and don't let any strangers in. I'll sing out when I want to come back in. You're on duty until four this afternoon. Mort Allen will show up then to relieve you. Don't leave until he gets here, OK?'

'Sure. I can handle it. No one will break in here, and if any outlaws do show up and try they'll get a load of buckshot around their ears. Is there anything else?'

'You know what to do. Just don't lose my three prisoners.' Turner went to the door, opened it and looked out at the street before turning to Walsh. 'Lock the door now, Art. I'll be back soon.' He paused, and then said: 'By the way, I've got Joey Donovan locked in the little cell off the kitchen – he's in protective custody. Give him anything he asks for, within reason, but don't turn him loose.'

Turner departed and walked along the street. There were few men around at that moment. He reached the general store, saw it was open for business and entered to find several men inside, crowded around Mort Preston, who was talking animatedly. The voices fell silent when the men noticed Turner. The sheriff walked up to the group and gazed intently at the storekeeper.

'Still trying to talk up a lynching, Mort?' he demanded.

'Is there a law against speaking out?' Preston demanded. 'My wife was murdered and nothing is being done about catching her killer.'

'You can say what you like, within reason, but the men listening to you will be mighty sorry if they take you at your word and begin to plot against law and order. Where did you get the idea from that Joey might have killed Martha? Did anyone say they saw him do it? Was he seen afterwards with a wad of greenbacks?'

'He was right here in the store at the time, and he ain't got all his senses.'

'That don't make him a killer. Joey thought the world of Martha. He wouldn't have hurt a hair of her head.' Turner shook his head emphatically.

'You never can tell when someone like him will kick over the traces and turn wild.' Preston drew a deep breath, restrained it for a moment, and then exhaled in a loud sigh. His eyes were hard and bright. His tongue flicked around his dry lips. 'I don't believe that yarn he spun about seeing a man in here wearing a gunny sack with holes cut in it. Nobody else saw the guy. I reckon if anyone was wearing a sack then it was Joey Donovan himself. It was quiet in the store. He could have hit Martha, grabbed the dough and ducked back into the store-room.'

'Sure he could have. So have you looked in there for the sack with the eyeholes in it? He had to hide it somewhere. And while we're talking about what happened to Martha you can tell me just where you were at the time of the murder.'

'Me?' Preston frowned. 'I was out delivering an order. That's why Martha was in the store. Joey Donovan was the only one who had the opportunity to do the killing. You should put pressure on him to make him talk. He's behind bars now, and that's where he should stay until you take him out and put a rope around his neck for killing my Martha.'

There was a chorus of agreement from the half dozen men present. Turner turned on them angrily.

'Ain't you got anything better to do than listen to Preston's poison?' he demanded. 'Go on, get out of here. I'm investigating a murder and I don't need you under my feet.'

The men departed, leaving Turner and Preston facing each other.

'Mort, do yourself a favour and keep your mouth shut about Martha's death,' Turner said.

'I'll say what I think. It was my wife that was killed.'

'All you'll do is muddy up the water, and then nobody will be able to sort out the problem. That's an order, Mort. You keep your mouth shut. I understand how you feel, but you've got to give us a chance to handle this our way.'

'I won't get any justice while Jim Donovan wears a star. He'll protect his brother.'

'You should know Jim better than that.' Turner gritted his teeth as a pang of pure agony shot through his big toe. 'If I hear another word out of you on this matter I'll throw you in jail and lose the key until I've arrested the killer. Keep your lip buttoned, Mort. I'll be watching you, so be warned.'

He started to turn away and then paused as a thought a struck him. 'All this talk about Joey Donovan, I nearly forgot to ask an important question.'

'What's that?'

'You said you were out delivering an order at the

time of the murder. So where were you?'

'I took a load of supplies to the Golden Slipper. I always deliver early there.'

'Who did you see when you got there?'

'Hatton the bartender let me in. He's always the first one in the saloon, and he was expecting me. I arranged the delivery the night before.'

'I've got the murder timed at eight,' Turner mused. 'What time did you get to the saloon?'

'I couldn't say exactly. I left here about a quarter to eight, and when I got back, Joey Donovan was on the street screeching about Martha being killed.' Sweat broke out on Preston's forehead and he cuffed it away. 'Why don't you check with Hatton? We had a few words while I was there. He'll remember.'

'I'll talk to him. I have to check out what you say. Now remember what I said. I don't want any more of your carping about the murder.'

Preston nodded and muttered under his breath. He looked into Turner's eyes.

'Is there anything else?' he demanded.

'Not right now. I'll come back to you if I think of something.'

Preston turned away and limped to the door of the storeroom. Turner watched him for a moment, and then called.

'You got your leg wound at Shiloh, didn't you, Mort?'

'That's right,' Preston replied without turning round.

'Does it pain you any?'

'Sure it does; mainly at night.'

'You have my sympathy. See you around, Mort.'

Turner went out to the street and headed for the freight office, his thoughts busy considering Mort Preston's words. He found Abe Williams in his office. The freighter sat back in his seat and placed his palms flat on the desk.

'I've told Jim Donovan all I know,' said Williams aggressively.

'Slow down, Abe,' Turner replied. 'You don't need to take that tone with me. If you're not careful you'll have me thinking you're guilty of something.'

'Why should you think that?' Williams put pressure on his hands, straightened his arms, and pushed his chair back until he was teetering on the two back legs.

'You're on the defensive, Abe, and that ain't good.'

'I can prove I was nowhere near the store when Martha was killed,' Williams declared.

'I don't doubt that. I haven't come to talk to you about the murder.'

Williams dropped his chair back on to four legs with a bang. He leaned forward and glared at Turner.

'Then what the hell do you want?' he demanded. 'I'm still smarting at the way Jim Donovan came in here throwing his weight around while I was talking business with a prospective employee.'

'Jim was only doing his job, and he was right to,'

Turner smiled. 'Your prospective employee turned out to be a wanted outlaw.'

'I didn't know that.'

'So let's forget about it. I'll overlook the fact that you seemed mighty guilty about something when I came in here. You went to the law office last evening and told Jim you saw Stomp Cullen sneaking into the saloon by the back door.'

'That's right. Ain't that what any law-abiding citizen should do if he sees a badman?'

'How did you happen to see him going into the saloon? You must have been prowling around that area after dark. What were you doing there? And how was it you saw Cullen and he didn't see you?'

'What are you saying, Sheriff? Are you accusing me of being up to no good last evening?'

'You're mighty touchy, Abe. Just simmer down and answer the question. I can't imagine what you would be doing at the back of the saloon in the dark.'

'What's so special about that? I was out looking around the rear of my freight yard. Someone has been out there the last few nights, and I was making sure I didn't lose anything. When I spotted two figures moving along the rear of the buildings fronting the street I got curious and tailed 'em. Mort Preston always keeps a lantern burning outside the back of his store, and that's how I recognized Stomp Cullen.'

'How'd you know him by sight?'

'I was in the Moundville bank a couple of years ago

when Cullen and his gang robbed it. He relieved me of the gold watch my father left me when he died. So when I saw him going into the back of the saloon I wanted to get my own back, and reported him to Donovan. But nothing came of it. Cullen must have given Donovan the slip.'

'And that's all there was to it, huh?'

'No more, no less. Am I in the clear?'

'I'll let you off this time,' Turner nodded.

He left the freight office and went to the saloon. Della was not there. Hatton was alone.

'Hello, Sheriff,' Hatton greeted. 'What can I do for you?'

'I need to ask you a couple of questions, but I'll have a whiskey first.'

'What's on your mind?' Hatton poured a whiskey and set it before Turner.

'You had an early delivery from the general store yesterday morning?'

'Sure. Mort Preston always delivers early. I like it that way. It gives me a chance to put everything away before the bar opens.'

'So tell me about yesterday morning.' Turner drank his whiskey at a gulp and set the glass back on the bar.

'There's nothing to tell. Preston brought the goods in as usual and I put them away.'

'What time did he make the delivery?'

'I got in around half past seven. I guess Preston turned up about fifteen minutes after that. He stood around talking some while I was putting the provisions away.'

'What time did he leave?'

'Around eight, I guess.'

'Thanks. That's all I wanta know. Is Della around?'

'No, she ain't. She left early this morning.'

'When she gets back tell her to drop in at the office. There are one or two things I need to talk to her about.'

'I'll do that, Sheriff. Do you want another drink?'

'I'd like one, but I've got things to do. See you later.'

Turner sauntered from the saloon and returned to the law office.

Donovan went down into the basin and slid into the stream that fed the creek. He waded upstream until he had passed the ranch house, intending to leave its cover to enter the house by the back door. He eased around a bend in the stream and came upon Frank Billings, crouched against the near bank, holding the outlaw's gun he had picked up. He was watching the house intently.

'Frank,' Donovan rapped. Billings jerked around, levelling his gun.

'Easy,' Donovan warned. 'Save your slugs for the outlaws.'

'Jim, where did you come from?' A big smile appeared on Billings' face. 'I'm sure glad to see you. Della is in the house, and Stomp Cullen, the outlaw,

111

is with her. Another outlaw rode in with Cullen, and he shot Rafe Carter off the roof.'

'I was on the rim. I saw what happened.' Donovan studied the side of the house. 'If Cullen is inside the house, I'm going in after him. I want you to stay here and shoot anyone coming around this side.'

'Hey, I'm not a gunman! I couldn't hit the side of the house even from here.'

'But you can make a noise, so stay alert, and don't shoot me if I happen to come into view. You should be safe here.'

'OK!' Billings was trembling, but he had a determined set to his chin, and looked at Donovan with a steady gaze. 'Don't get yourself killed, Jim.'

'I'll do the best I can to stay alive,' Donovan replied. 'Stay here no matter what you see or hear. I need a clear field to take on Cullen.'

He patted Billings' shoulder reassuringly and went on; climbing out of the stream when he judged that he could not be seen from the house. He reached a rear corner of the building, cocked his pistol and peered around the back yard. The place was deserted. He paused for some moments, listening intently. The silence was overwhelming. His heart thudded and his pulses raced. He was excited at the thought of getting to grips with Stomp Cullen.

As he moved around the corner to head for the back door of the house he heard the sound of hoofs pounding the hardpan of the front yard. His caution fled as the import of it came to him and he ran along the back of the house to the far corner. When he looked out towards the corral he saw a rider galloping away around it. He recognized Cullen and fired two shots, but the outlaw was low in his saddle and the shooting had no visible effect. Cullen passed out of pistol range. Donovan ran along the side of the house, recalling that more horses were standing outside the front door.

Della appeared at the front corner of the house and stood gazing after the outlaw. Donovan called to her and she came running towards him, her face ashen, eyes filled with shock.

'Jim, where did you come from?' she demanded, and dissolved into tears. He put a comforting arm around her shoulders.

'You've got some questions to answer, Della,' he said in her ear.

'Have you seen Frank Billings?' she countered.

'He's safe – hiding in the stream. I'm gonna take out after Cullen.'

He left her, then went to the front of the house and collected a horse standing there with trailing reins. He swung into the saddle and spurred the animal. Hoofs thudded on the hard ground as he galloped around the corral and set out after the fleeing outlaw.

Donovan knew there were only two exits in the direction they were riding. Cullen passed one almost immediately, a game trail that meandered up the west wall and was too steep for a horse to negotiate.

Donovan pushed his horse to its limit, and began to overhaul the outlaw.

Cullen evidently knew all about the exits, for he headed directly for the one to the north. Donovan could see the spot ahead, where a landslip many years before had eased the angle of the sloping wall, and the hoofs of horses and wildlife thereafter had marked out a difficult access track to the upper range outside the basin.

Cullen kept riding, and began the ascent to the rim, driving his horse recklessly upwards. He was more than three parts of the way to the rim when Donovan lifted his rifle and aimed at him. Donovan centred the foresight on Cullen and squeezed the trigger. Cullen jerked as the bullet struck him in the body and then fell forward over the horse's neck.

For some moments Cullen clung to the horse as the animal continued its upward rush. Donovan raised the rifle again, determined to put an end to Cullen's criminal career. But as he drew a bead on Cullen his horse slipped, its back legs crumpling, and Cullen lost his balance and fell sideways out of the saddle. The horse rolled a couple of times and tried desperately to regain its feet, but the incline was too steep and the animal fell to the bottom, hoofs thrashing. Cullen disappeared from sight.

Donovan dismounted and started up the slope on foot. He could not see Cullen. There were rocks on the upper slope, and he would have to check them one by one for the outlaw's position. A sudden movement up near the rim attracted his gaze and he caught a glimpse of the gang boss struggling to climb over the rim of the basin. Before he could lift his pistol, Cullen clawed his way free, slipped out of sight, and was gone. . . .

EIGHT

The cells behind the law office in Lodestone were silent and still when Art Walsh entered to check on the prisoners in his care. Shap Kelly was sitting on the foot of his bunk, gazing into space but seeing nothing of his surroundings as he wondered how he could get out of his present situation. In the next cell, Elroy Johnson was lying on his bunk, sweating, his eyes closed, his body racked with the pain of his wound; Noll Watson was stretched out on his bunk in the end cell, chatting to Johnson, who ignored him.

Johnson lifted his head to peer at the jailer, and did a double-take. 'Art Walsh,' he declared. 'What in hell are you doing in here? You're the wrong side of the bars, ain't you?'

'Not me, Elroy. I gave up the bad life years ago. I can sleep with an easy mind these nights. I got a good life now.'

'How's your wife?' Johnson inquired. 'You've been married five years now, huh?'

116

'Nearly six,' Walsh corrected.

'How about helping an old friend?'

'How?' Walsh felt uneasiness trickle through his mind.

'I'm in a real bad spot right now,' Johnson replied, 'and you're in a good position to help me out. All you've got to do is unlock these cells doors and we'll wave goodbye to this burg.'

'Hell, I couldn't do that! The sheriff would know straight off that I did it.'

'I seem to remember keeping my mouth shut about you when I was sent to prison.' Johnson grimaced. 'One good turn deserves another. But if you don't want to help out an old friend then let's bring your wife into this, Art. You wouldn't want her to meet with an accident sometime in the near future, huh?'

'I didn't say I wouldn't help you,' Walsh responded. 'How could I get you out of here?'

'When you get off duty,' Johnson said easily, 'come back when the town is quiet and Mort Allen is here. Get the drop on him, tie him up and then turn us loose.'

'Allen will see it's me,' Walsh protested.

'Not if you wear a gunny sack like the man who killed Martha did. Say you'll do it this evening, Art. You won't regret it.'

'I'll do it under protest, Elroy,' Walsh nodded. 'Wait till the town quietens down.'

'Now you're talking, old friend,' Johnson replied

117

with a grin.

Walsh grimaced and tried the doors of the cells, found them securely locked and went back into the front office. Kelly waited until he heard the sound of the connecting door being locked before he spoke.

'Do you think you can trust him, Johnson?'

'Sure I'm sure. I've got enough on Walsh to have him thrown in jail for ten years. He'll be back later. Now let me get some sleep or I won't be up to making a run for it when the time comes.'

'Did Cullen say what his plans were before he took off?'

'The hell he did. He plays his cards close to his vest.'

'Where did he go when he left you?'

'He said he was going out to my place. The rest of his gang are waiting there for him. But he was gonna check out his sister's new ranch first. It's close by.'

'Are they coming into town to hit the bank?'

'That was the plan, but Cullen got the idea it would pay more to hijack a silver shipment from the big mine. That's why you were trying to get a job with the freight line, huh?'

'I wasn't told anything except to get a job hauling freight.' Kelly shook his head. 'So that's what it was all about, huh?'

'You know Cullen,' Johnson shrugged. 'He's willing to try anything once. He'd rob his own mother if he had to.'

'I don't like the idea of stealing silver. Robbing

banks is OK – the dough can be spent anywhere – but where do you sell off a load of silver?'

'Back to the mine you stole it from.' Johnson laughed, despite the pain he was suffering, and closed his eyes, intent on getting some sleep. . . .

Cullen squirmed over the rim of the basin and flopped down into cover. Donovan's bullet had gouged his right side just above the hip and he was bleeding. He listened to the fading echoes of the shooting, decided there would be no immediate pursuit, and checked his wound. He ripped off his shirt, padded it over the wound and used his belt to hold it in place. Then he pushed himself to his feet, peered over the rim into the basin and saw Donovan riding back toward the ranch house.

Donovan was out of pistol shot, and Cullen gazed at him like a mountain lion regarding a potential meal, but he was not given to wishful thinking and looked around to get his bearings. It was a six-mile hike to Johnson's run-down ranch, and the sooner he reached it the better. He stifled his thoughts and feelings and set out, pushing one foot in front of the other with great effort. . . .

Della stood in front of the ranch house in the basin, racked with worry. She heard the distant shooting, and knew she was in for some grief whatever the outcome. If Donovan had killed her brother she would suffer for the rest of her life, for blood was thicker than water, and if Cullen had killed Donovan she would miss the big deputy because she had always been more than half in love with him. She waited in a ferment of fearful anticipation, hoping that Cullen would escape from the basin before Donovan caught up with him.

When a horse showed up in the distance she shaded her eyes with her hat and studied the rider. Her heart seemed to lurch when she recognized Donovan, who came trotting around the corral and reined up in front of the house. His face was grim as he stepped down from the saddle.

'Did you get Cullen?' Billings demanded.

'He got away, but I winged him.' Donovan glanced at Della and saw relief show momentarily on her face. 'Have you got Carter's body ready for taking to town?' he asked Billings. 'I need to get moving. I'll push on with Della. You can bring Carter along. I want to get a posse and go for Cullen.'

'I'll handle things here,' Billings said. 'But first I want to thank you, Jim, for saving my life. That outlaw was gonna gun me down in cold blood when you shot him.'

'Forget it, Frank,' Donovan replied. 'It's all part of the job. Are you ready to leave, Della? I need to get to town fast. Cullen is wounded, and I won't get a better chance of nailing him.'

Della did not reply. She crossed to where her white mare was standing and swung into the saddle. Donovan set out for the trail leading out of the basin and pushed the horse into a lope. Della followed him closely, staying behind him while they negotiated the trail out of the basin. Donovan's horse was waiting patiently on the ledge where he had left it on the way in and he transferred to it. When they reached level ground and were jogging in the direction of Lodestone, Della came up alongside him.

'How are you feeling now?' he asked, glancing at her intently. He had stifled his personal feelings for her years before, when his interest had first become apparent. Now, as far as he was concerned, she was merely another of the people living in the town where he helped to uphold the law. His way of life was such that he did not think he could maintain a relationship with a woman. His demanding job over-filled his life as it was, and he had his brother to watch out for; he was aware that there was no one else in the whole wide world to take care of Joey.

'I've got something to tell you, Jim,' Della said in a low tone. 'You're suspicious of me where Cullen is concerned. I can see it in your eyes. The truth is—' she paused and drew a deep breath. 'He's my brother. We went our separate ways years ago, when he first broke the law, and I haven't seen him much over the last ten years. He showed up at the saloon last week, and I sent him to my horse ranch to keep him out of your way. I was hoping he would ride on after a few days.'

'He's your brother?' Donovan shot a glance at her set face. He sighed. 'So that's it!'

'We don't pick our family,' Della observed, shrugging her slim shoulders.

Donovan shook his head. 'Cullen is a real bad 'un. He's big trouble for you, brother or not. He'll drag you down to his level, no matter what you think of him.'

'I realized that earlier today. I warned him to quit while he was ahead, but he just laughed. I hope you catch him. He's no longer kin to me.'

'Now you're talking my language.' Donovan glanced around, checking the skyline. 'Did he give any hint about his future plans?'

'No. And I don't want to know. Just go after him.'

They rode on in silence. Donovan considered what she had told him. He sympathized with her, and some of his old feelings for her struggled to the surface of his mind, but he didn't like the way his thoughts were turning and tried to reject them. However, looking at Della's face, he could judge the extent to which she was concerned, and a wave of unaccustomed emotion assailed him. Acting on an impulse, he reached out a hand and touched her shoulder. She looked up at him quickly and he saw tears shimmering in her eyes. 'He's no longer my brother. I saw him for what he was when poor Rafe Carter was shot for no reason at all.'

'I'm sorry for you, Della,' he said, his voice husky, his throat constricted. 'I don't know why I should have thought you were somehow in cahoots with Cullen. But I could tell you were lying when I asked if he had visited you in the saloon, and naturally I thought the worst. But him being your brother puts a different face on it. I've got to go after him, and I don't doubt I'll have to kill him.'

'You must do your duty,' she said harshly. 'I wouldn't ask you to go easy on him. He's a killer, a mad dog, and he's got to be stopped. Poor Rafe Carter was no danger to him; he was a decent, hard-working young man, and was shot like a wild animal, for no reason at all.'

They travelled in silence for the rest of the trip to town. Donovan was thoughtful, aware that he was suddenly feeling different about this woman. He longed to comfort her, but was afraid of easing his manner. He could never think any further than his brother. Joey needed him – would always have to rely on him – and there was no room for anyone else in their constricted world.

He was relieved when they reached Lodestone. He reined up in front of the law office. Della kept riding, and Donovan called after her.

'I'll come and see you later. I should be back by morning. Take care of yourself, Della.'

She twisted in her saddle, gazed at him for a moment and then her lips pulled into a thin line. 'I've been taking care of myself for a long time now,' she replied. 'But thanks for your concern, Jim. Come and see me when you get back, and bear in mind that I shall worry about you until this dreadful business is over.'

He stepped down from his saddle and stood watching her progress along the street. A voice called his name and he turned swiftly to see the sheriff opening the door of the office.

'Glad you're back, Jim. Did you have any luck?'

Donovan suppressed a sigh, took a last look at Della and then entered the office. Turner's face showed a series of emotions as he listened to Donovan's report.

'I'll have to ride out again,' Donovan concluded. 'Cullen was afoot the last time I saw him, and if he doesn't steal a horse I should get him. I'll need a fresh horse and a posse. I haven't seen more than half a dozen of Cullen's gang, and we know he runs at least a dozen hardcases. The rest of them will be hiding out somewhere in the hills, and the sooner we get them the better. Has Joey had a good meal today? We're gonna have to have a rethink about him, Dan. It ain't right, him being cooped up in the jail all day long.'

'He said he'd wait to eat until you got back. I wish I knew what to do with him. It's a pity we can't find a good widow woman who'd keep an eye on him for you.'

'That would never work,' Donovan mused. 'I need some food so I'll take him along to the diner now. Organize a posse for me, Dan – about six men. I'll be ready to ride out in around half an hour. Have you made any progress in Martha's murder? We've got to get something going in that case. Someone in town must know something.'

'I've asked around but nothing has come to light. You better get moving if you wanta pull out again in thirty minutes.'

Donovan fetched Joey out of the cell, and the youth was like a foal turned out to pasture. He talked incessantly and danced around Donovan as they went along the sidewalk. Donovan shook his head. He knew it was wrong for his brother to be penned up in a cell all day, but there seemed to be no solution to the problem.

'Stop running around like a chicken with its head cut off,' he reproved, and Joey came obediently to his side. 'Have you remembered anything else about Martha's murder? I want to get the man who killed her.'

'I don't like to think about it,' replied Joey, 'but I can't help it. Everything is going round in my head, and it's all mixed up. I feel there is something else I want to tell you, but I can't pick it out.'

'Is it about the man wearing the gunny sack?' Donovan halted and reached out to grasp Joey's shoulder. 'Let's go over it again, Joey. Tell me everything that happened when Martha was killed. Picture the killer standing there. Did he look familiar to you? Was it a townsman you saw?'

'It's no good, Jim. My mind ain't working right. I don't know who it was. He looked so strange with a sack on his head. I didn't think of looking at him real good. All I could see was the sack. I guess he wore it because he didn't wanta be recognized.'

'Which means he was a local man,' Donovan mused. 'OK, Joey, forget it now. Let's get some chow. And we've got to get moving because I'm riding out again shortly.'

Donovan was impatient to get after Cullen but Joey would not be pushed along, and when Donovan tried to move him from the dining table after they had eaten he shook his head obstinately and spilled a glass of water over a passing waitress.

'I don't want to go back in the cell,' he declared, using a tone that Donovan knew full well. 'I ain't done anything wrong, and you lock me up like I was a badman.'

'It's for your own good, Joey,' Donovan grimaced. 'Something bad might happen to you if you are out on the street. Come on now. I've got to ride out.'

Joey got up and slouched to the door, and Donovan had to shorten his stride to stay abreast of him. When they entered the office the sheriff stood up from his desk.

'I've arranged for a posse,' he said. 'It'll be waiting for you at the livery barn. Come on, Joey, I'll put you back in your cell.'

Turner led Joey into the kitchen. When he returned he dumped the cell keys on the desk and sat down again. Donovan turned to the street door.

'I've got to be riding,' he said, and departed in a hurry.

Mort Allen entered the office at that moment and

Turner prepared to leave.

'Just keep the front and back doors locked,' he told the jailer. 'Don't let in anyone you don't know. Joey Donovan is locked in the kitchen cell. Don't let him out. I've got some more questions to ask around town so I'll leave you to it.'

Turner departed. Allen sat down at the desk and took a pack of playing cards from a pocket. He cleared a space then dealt the cards to play a game of solitaire. Later, when he turned sleepy, he lounged back in the chair and closed his eyes.

Art Walsh was highly nervous when he returned to the law office later. He peered through the front window and saw Mort Allen asleep at the desk. Walsh glanced around the street. Shadows were drawing in and no one was around. He steeled himself for what would be an ordeal, unlocked the door of the office and entered, pausing only to pull a gunny sack over his head. He had cut the eye holes too wide apart and could see though only one of them. He drew his pistol and approached the desk, jarring it accidently when he reached it.

Allen started up uneasily but did not awaken. Walsh struck him a heavy blow on the head with the barrel of his gun and Allen slumped forward, his face striking the desk. He lay motionless. Walsh snatched up the jail keys and hurried into the cell block. His hands shook as he unlocked the cell doors.

Johnson slid off his bunk and staggered out of the cell. He snatched the keys from Walsh and then took his gun. Kelly and Watson joined him and hurried to the back door. Walsh accompanied them, and when they left the jail by the back door they separated. Walsh hurried home to his wife, hoping that he had not seriously injured Allen.

NINE

Cullen staggered along in the direction of Johnson's derelict horse ranch, hunched over and hurting from the bullet gouge across the top of his right hip. He needed a horse, but there were no ranches in the area and he walked on doggedly, planning what he would do to Jim Donovan if they met again. He covered a couple of miles before falling on his face, and lay as dead until he heard the thud of approaching hoofs. He rolled on to his back, grunting in pain, and, seeing a rider approaching from the left, ducked down in the tall grass. But he knew he had been seen, and sat up as the rider arrived.

'Howdy,' the man called reining in beside him. 'You've been hurt. What happened?'

'I was shot out of my saddle,' Cullen declared, 'and my horse was stole.'

'Are you bad hurt?' The man dismounted. He was young; dressed in range clothes. He turned towards Cullen and then froze, finding himself looking into the muzzle of Cullen's gun.

'I need your horse,' Cullen said, and fired. The slug took the man in the centre of his chest. He fell backward, uttering a cry of shock, and dropped lifeless to the ground. His horse started nervously at the sound, moved away several paces, then halted and began to graze.

Cullen staggered to his feet and holstered his gun. He looked around. Sweat was running down his face. He went to the horse, took up the reins and hauled himself into the saddle. He looked down unemotionally at the dead stranger and then took in his surroundings with a quick glance around. He picked out the direction of Lodestone, swung the horse around and spurred it. He had to go back to town to see the doctor.

He kept a close watch on the trail ahead, fearing that Donovan would get to town, collect a posse and return to the scene of the shooting. Three miles on, he spotted a bunch of riders heading his way and rode into cover. He sat hunched over in the saddle, groaning each time he drew breath. He watched the riders sweep by at a gallop and recognized Donovan in the lead, a law star glittering on his chest. Cullen's eyes narrowed. He decided to see the doctor and then become an uninvited guest at the Golden Slipper until he had rested up.

He approached Lodestone cautiously and rode in behind the buildings fronting the street. He knew the town pretty well, and left the horse standing at the rear of the doctor's house. He tried the back door, which opened to his touch, and entered, walking to the front of the building where the doctor's office was situated. The door of the office was ajar and he pushed it wide.

A good-looking older woman, tall and slender, with an attractive face framed by corn-coloured hair, was sitting at a desk in a corner reading through a sheaf of medical notes. She looked up as Cullen stepped into the office, and then arose from the desk.

'You've been hurt,' she said, noting blood on his shirt. 'Come and sit down on the couch. I'm afraid the doctor isn't here at the moment, but I'm his wife, Mrs Hardy, and I am a trained nurse.'

'I was nicked by a bullet,' Cullen said. 'I don't think it's serious, but it needs cleaning up.'

'Take off your shirt and I'll see what needs to be done.'

Cullen removed his hat and his shirt. Mrs Hardy examined the wound and then fetched water and bandages. She cleansed the wound, applied some salve and bandaged it.

'It's not serious, and should heal quickly if you keep it clean,' she told him. 'You're a stranger in town. Will you be staying long?'

'I hadn't planned to, but I'll stick around until I've healed.'

'Then come in and see the doctor in two days, Mr. . . ?'

'Talbot, Ma'am – Frank Talbot.' Cullen replaced his shirt. 'What do I owe you?'

'Come and see the doctor in two days and you can settle with him.'

'Thank you kindly.' Cullen picked up his hat and departed.

He left the horse where it stood and skirted the rear of the buildings until he reached an alley almost directly opposite the Golden Slipper. He looked around the street. It was late afternoon and there was a sprinkling of townsfolk on the sidewalks. He decided it was safe to move around, and sauntered across the street to enter an alley at the side of the saloon.

A small window adjacent to a side door gave him the opportunity to look into the saloon, and he grimaced when he saw his sister, Della, standing at the bar talking to the sheriff. Their conversation seemed to be serious, and he wondered if she was giving the lawman the lowdown on her notorious brother. He smiled and turned away. Perhaps it would not be a good idea to reveal his presence at this time.

He went to the far end of the alley and walked along the rear of the buildings to the freight yard. There was no activity there. A big freight wagon stood inside, and there were tarp-covered stacks dotted in a corner. A man was swilling down a fenced area in a corner, where several mules were feeding. Cullen turned to the adjacent house and tried the back door. He cursed when he found it locked, so he entered the alley at the side of the house. He walked to the street end.

He felt naked as he stepped out on to the sidewalk and made for the office door. Although he thought he would not easily be recognized, he did not like to attract attention to himself, and his hand was close to the butt of his gun as he entered the privacy of the building. He went into the freight office and confronted Abe Williams, who was seated at his desk. Williams looked up, his mouth agape when he recognized Cullen. He sprang to his feet.

'What in hell are you doing here?' he demanded.

'Keep your hair on!' Cullen replied. 'I was in a bit of trouble today, and this is the only place I thought I might be welcome.'

'You've got a nerve! I've got Kelly and Johnson and Watson here.'

'The hell you say! Where are they?'

'Upstairs in a bedroom. They're gonna ride out to Johnson's place after dark.'

'What are they doing here? I dropped Johnson and Kelly off outside town earlier today. Kelly was told to see you about driving a wagon, and Johnson needed to see the doctor.'

'That damn deputy, Donovan, arrested Johnson in the doc's house, and then came in here while I was talking to Kelly and arrested him. How did Donovan know they were in town? The deal between us was supposed to be a secret. There's been trouble in town for a couple of days now. Martha Preston, the storekeep's wife, was murdered and robbed in the store. One of your men, Sam Rouse, was in the store about the time it happened, and he killed a couple of men as he rode out. Donovan took out after him, and brought him back dead.'

'I don't know a damn thing about any of this,' said Cullen furiously. 'If Kelly and Johnson were in jail then how did they escape?'

'Johnson knew the jailer from way back. They want to lie low here until dark. I've got to provide three horses for them.'

'I'm here for the same reason,' Cullen admitted. 'I had some bad luck earlier, when Donovan showed up at a ranch I was visiting. I'll have to do something about him. He's getting in my hair. Take me to Johnson and the other two. I need to talk to them, and when you get the horses later bring one for me.'

'We're gonna have to think some more about stealing a silver shipment,' Williams said. 'I can't afford to use one of your men as a driver. They're too well known around here. I'll get someone I can trust, and let you know when it's arranged.'

'We'll be out at Johnson's place for a spell,' Cullen mused. 'Send word to me there, and be careful how you handle it.'

Williams was not happy as he showed Cullen up to the bedroom where Johnson, Kelly, and Watson were hiding.

Donovan led his posse out to Della's new ranch in

134

the basin, heading for the place on the rim where he had last seen Cullen. He sensed that he had the gang boss at a disadvantage, and was keen to take the outlaw. With six experienced posse men at his back he was confident of succeeding.

When they reached the rim of the basin, Donovan pinpointed the spot where Cullen had disappeared. He dismounted and walked around, looking for sign. He found the spot where the outlaw had left the basin and checked the direction Cullen had taken. He soon realized that the outlaw had been walking towards Johnson's spread, and he called his posse men to prepare to ride on.

Hank Root, a stock handler in town, spotted a body lying on the ground and alerted Donovan. They dismounted around the dead man.

'It's Johnny Fry,' Root declared. 'He rides for Leather Face Jones. Now who the hell would wanta shoot Johnny?'

'Cullen,' Donovan said. 'He needed a horse.'

'I saw Johnny in town earlier,' Root mused. 'He said he came in to pick up some gear for Leather Face.'

Donovan examined the body – saw that Fry had been killed with a single shot through the heart. He straightened and checked the ground; he followed the prints to where Fry's horse had moved on some yards, and then found the tracks heading towards town.

'It looks like Cullen is heading for Lodestone,' he

said. 'He probably needs to see Doc Hardy. We're not far from Johnson's place now so we'll take the time to visit it. The rest of Cullen's gang may be there, and if they are we'll do well to put them out of business. Mount up and we'll push on.'

They continued, silent and determined. Johnson's small ranch was only a few miles ahead, and in no time they'd halted and dismounted in cover at a spot which gave them a view of the place. The ranch consisted of a cabin, a barn and a corral. Donovan studied the dilapidated horse ranch, and saw five horses in the small corral. Two men were seated on a bench against the front wall of the cabin and another was standing in the doorway of the barn, holding a rifle.

Donovan knew the place should be deserted, and was elated by the discovery.

'It looks like we're in luck,' he told the posse men. 'Five horses in the corral and three men in view around the place. We can count on two more being in the cabin. Let's split into two groups. I'll go in with three of you from the front and the others can cut 'em off from behind. We'll get a look at them to check who they are, but I'm pretty sure they're the rest of Cullen's gang. If they start shooting then pile in. They'll try to run and won't surrender, so shoot to kill. OK, Hank, you take three men and cover the rear. Stay out of sight until you hear me shooting, then close in fast and don't let anyone get away.'

Hank Root led three of the posse men away in a circle to get behind the buildings. Donovan gave them time to get into position. He could feel a small fluttering of excitement in his chest as he told his men to mount up. They rode at a canter towards the cabin, spreading out as they drew nearer, and held their guns, prepared for resistance.

The two men seated on the bench were obviously relaxing. One of them appeared to be asleep, but the other heard the beat and thud of approaching hoofs and stood up to stare at the newcomers. Donovan saw the watching man kick at the outstretched legs of his sleeping companion, who jerked and scrambled to his feet, took one look at the approaching riders and ran into the cabin. Donovan cocked his gun.

The man standing by the bench was suddenly galvanized into action. He pulled his holstered pistol and lifted it, dropping to one knee as he took aim at Donovan's group. The three posse men opened fire. The outlaw got off a shot, and Donovan heard the crackle of a closely passing slug. Then gun thunder broke the heavy silence and a string of echoes fled across the rough terrain. The man was hit, threw down his gun, twisted around and fell on his face.

A gun fired at them from the open doorway of the cabin. Donovan eased his horse to the left and kept moving in, returning fire. His posse men fired at the front window when a gun began banging from the aperture, and a man suddenly fell forward, head and one shoulder coming through the glassless window. He dropped a pistol and hung lifeless over the window ledge.

Shooting hammered from the rear of the cabin. Donovan rode up to the doorway. There was no more resistance from inside the cabin. He jumped down from his saddle and ran into the building, gun levelled. Two men lay on the earthen floor. One had been firing at Donovan from the front doorway. The other was lying by the back door, which was open, and Donovan could see a couple of posse men approaching the rear of the cabin. The shooting dwindled away. Donovan yelled to the posse men out back, and then stepped into the rear doorway. Hank Root was dismounting close by, his gun smoking.

Donovan saw the outlaw guard lying prone in front of the barn, and another outlaw was stretched out in the open, caught as he fled from the cabin. Root stopped to check the bodies, and then came to where Donovan was standing.

'That went well,' Root observed. 'The two here are dead. How did you get on out front?'

'One dead out front and two dead inside the cabin. That ties up with the number of horses in the corral. It looks like Cullen just lost his gang.'

'And you reckon he rode into Lodestone?'

'I reckon he needed to see the doc. Let's get back to town. With any luck we'll catch Cullen unawares.'

'What about these dead outlaws?' Root demanded.

'I'll send the undertaker out tomorrow with a wagon and he can tote them in.' Donovan was elated with his success. He went to his horse, mounted, and led the posse back to town.

Sheriff Turner learned nothing as he went around town asking questions. No one except Joey Donovan had seen Martha Preston's killer. Abe Williams had nothing further to say about almost hiring an outlaw as a freight driver. Turner went on to the saloon and questioned Della about the alleged visit of the outlaw gang boss. She denied knowing Cullen. The sheriff gave up and returned to the law office as shadows began to slip into odd corners around the long main street.

He knocked at the door of the office, and when there was no immediate reply he kicked the door impatiently. He was tired and his joints were aching intolerably. There was no reply so he tried the door, which opened at his touch. He entered to discover Mort Allen lying across the desk, and saw a trickle of blood that had spilled across some of the scattered papers around him. Allen was dead. Turner was stunned, paralyzed by shock.

He went to the cells, opened the connecting door, and paused to look around. He saw the doors of Kelly's and Johnson's cells standing open, and the back door was ajar. He went into the kitchen and saw Joey asleep on the bunk in the small cell. He went through the cell block to the back door, looked outside but saw nothing and then closed the door and bolted it.

He examined the locks on both cell doors. They

had not been broken. He looked around for the cell keys and could not find them in the office. He sat down on a chair and stared in total shock at Allen's body.

Full darkness had settled over the town when Donovan and the posse returned. They reined up outside the doctor's office and Donovan swung out of his saddle. He stepped on to the sidewalk, and then paused to look at the posse men.

'You did a real good job,' he told them.

'What about Cullen?' Root asked. 'Do you want any help taking him?'

'No. I can handle it. You can stand down now. Thanks for your help. I'll see you later.'

The posse men rode along the street to the livery barn. Donovan rapped on the door of the doctor's house and it was opened by Doc Hardy himself.

'Jim!' Hardy exclaimed. 'I was about to pay the law office a visit. I was out of town this afternoon when a man came in and saw my wife. He had a bullet wound in his back. Nothing serious, she said. But she didn't like the look of him. She patched him up and told him to see me in a couple of days. He said he would, but from what she said about him I doubt he'll come back.'

'I shot Cullen, the outlaw, earlier today, and he headed for town. I guess he was coming to see you.' Donovan described Cullen, and the doctor nodded.

'That sounds like the man Mrs Hardy saw. She described him in detail. He went out the back door, but she watched the street, and a few moments later she saw him head into the alley beside the saloon.'

'That figures.' Donovan nodded. 'I won't come in now, Doc. I'm in a hurry. I think I know where Cullen might be.'

He turned away and crossed the street to the saloon, shouldered through the batwings and walked the length of the bar towards Della's office, waving a hand to Hatton, the bartender, in passing. He reached the office door, drew his pistol and then thrust the door open. He paused in the doorway. Della was seated at her desk, and she was alone.

'Jim!' She jumped up and came to him, holding out her hands.

Donovan avoided her hands and holstered his gun. 'Where is he?' he demanded.

She gazed at him and a frown marred her smooth forehead. 'Where's who?' she countered.

'Cullen.' Donovan explained what had happened when he had ridden out with the posse.

'You're wrong, Jim, if you think Cullen came back here. I haven't seen him or I would have reported him to the sheriff.' She saw the expression that crossed his face and clutched at his arm. 'You've got to believe me, Jim. After what happened out at the basin today I wouldn't lift a finger to help him. I'm disgusted with him. Feel free to search the place if you don't believe me. I've got nothing to hide.'

'If he didn't come in here then where did he go?' Donovan frowned. 'He might have left town again,

141

and if he is heading for Johnson's spread then he's gonna get the shock of his life. We caught the rest of his gang there – five men – and shot them to hell; killed all of them.'

Della looked at him with horror in her eyes. Donovan heaved a sigh.

'I'm sorry to come in here with accusations,' he said, aware of his rising feelings for her and trying ruthlessly to smother them. 'I'll take you at your word, Della. I'd better report to the sheriff. We'll start a search of the town for Cullen. See you later.'

He departed, heading for the law office. The door was ajar, and he found Turner seated inside, gazing at Allen's body. The sheriff did not reply when Donovan, badly shocked, spoke to him, and panic struck Donovan when he thought of Joey. He ran into the kitchen, and was overwhelmed with relief at the sight of his brother sleeping peacefully in the small cell. When he looked into the cell block and saw the empty cells he sighed heavily.

Donovan went back to Joey's cell. His brother stirred, opened his eyes and sat up.

'Did you get any badmen?' he demanded.

'The posse killed five of them,' Donovan told him. 'But Kelly and Johnson have gone again.'

'I've remembered something,' Joey declared. 'I heard Preston tell Martha he would kill her if he found out she was seeing another man. That's how he put it. And he was madder than a wet hen. I was helping in the store the morning I heard their voices.'

142

Donovan gazed at his brother and decided that he was telling the truth. 'When did Mort say that?' he demanded.

'It was last week sometime,' Joey smiled wanly. 'And Martha lied to him when she said she wasn't seeing anyone because I saw her several times with Abe Williams. One time they were kissing in the freight yard. I was watching them that day, and I heard Williams tell Martha she should leave Preston and go away with him.'

Donovan studied Joey's expression. He drew a deep breath, restrained it for a moment and then heaved a long sigh.

'You'll cause a lot of trouble if you're telling me lies, Joey,' he warned. 'I'll ask you again – are you telling the truth about seeing Williams and Martha together?'

'I'm not lying, Jim. I'm telling you what I saw.'

'And who did you see when Martha was killed? Who was wearing that sack over his head? Was it Abe Williams or Mort Preston?'

'I can't say!' Joey shook his head. 'I was so frightened when Martha was hit on the head.'

'Was he tall, like Abe Williams, or skinny like Mort Preston?' Donovan persisted.

'I don't remember.' Joey shook his head. He went back to the bunk and threw himself face down on it, his body racked by a bout of convulsive sobbing.

Donovan turned away and went back into the office to see the sheriff getting to his feet.

'I had a real bad shock when I came in and found Mort stretched out like that,' Turner said. 'I'll get Doc over here.'

Donovan made a report on the posse's action. 'I've got something I want to follow up right away,' he ended. 'Will you carry on here for a spell?'

'I'm all right now,' Turner replied. 'I'll be here until you get back.'

Donovan nodded and departed. There were many things he wanted to check on and didn't know where to start. But he wanted to talk to Mort Preston, and made his way to the general store.

He was entering the store when the crash of a shot shattered the silence. He dived in through the doorway for cover, thinking he was under attack, and his gun was in his hand when he fell across some sacks inside.

TEN

Donovan got to his feet and peered out at the street, staying within the shelter of the store doorway. He heard gun echoes fading but could not pinpoint their direction. His gaze shifted to the law office and something clicked in his brain. He ran towards the jail, fearing that something might have happened to Joey. He shouldered open the law office door and pulled up short when he saw the sheriff lying on the floor by the desk. Turner was dead, a bullet in his chest. Donovan turned like a man in a nightmare and ran into the kitchen.

A faint trace of gunsmoke hung in a pungent cloud in the small room. He saw Joey lying on his bunk in the cell, a patch of blood staining his shirt front. Donovan's hand shook as he unlocked the cell door. He examined Joey, found him unconscious and bleeding from a chest wound.

Donovan did what he could to stem the bleeding. He stared at his brother with disbelief throbbing in his mind. His thoughts seemed frozen, but a name stood out bright and clear: Mort Preston. The storekeeper had threatened to shoot Joey.

Donovan checked the back door, which led into an alley. The lock was broken. A footstep sounded in the front office and Doc Harvey called out. Donovan called the doctor through and stood by while Joey was examined, waiting in a timeless, torturous void, hoping that Joey was not too badly hurt. The doctor turned to him eventually, and Donovan barely heard his voice.

'He's in a bad way, Jim. I need to operate immediately. Bring him over to my office. I'll go and prepare.'

Donovan nodded, feeling as though he was caught up in a living nightmare. He followed the doctor to the street door. A group of townsmen were standing on the sidewalk, their combined voices a high-pitched, unintelligible babble. Questions were shouted at him. He ignored them; shouted over them.

'Four of you come in. I want to get Joey over to the doc's office.'

Four volunteers rushed into the office. Donovan pulled a table from under the side window. He led the way into the kitchen and paused at Joey's cell door.

'Two of you pick him up carefully and bring him into the office,' he instructed.

Questions flew back and forth as Joey's unconscious figure was taken into the front office and placed on the table, which was then carried out to the street before being moved in a slow procession to the doctor's office. Doc Hardy took control, ushering the crowding townsmen out of his office. He placed a hand on Donovan's shoulder.

'Go and get yourself a drink, Jim,' he suggested. 'There's nothing useful you can do here and I don't want you underfoot. Give me an hour, and by that time I might have some news for you.'

'I have got things to do, Doc,' Donovan replied. He turned away. 'See you later.'

His mind sharpened as he reached the street. He ignored the crowd and set off for the freight office. He almost bumped into Della on the sidewalk, not seeing her, and as he stepped around her she put out a restraining hand.

'Jim, have you got a minute?' she asked.

'Della! I'm sorry. I didn't recognize you. My mind is on other things at the moment.'

'I heard Joey was shot. How is he?'

'I don't know yet. Doc told me to see him later.'

'You look all-in, Jim. You've been pushing yourself hard lately, and the sheriff is no help to you.'

'The sheriff is dead – shot. I want to find Elroy Johnson, and your brother is somewhere around. Have you seen him?'

'I said I'd tell you if I ever set eyes on him again.' She turned abruptly to leave but he reached out and grasped her arm.

'Don't rush off, Della. I'm sorry. I'm still shocked

147

by what's happened to Joey.'

Della remained silent.

'There will be some big changes around here when this present trouble is over,' Donovan said slowly, and laughed mirthlessly; a low, harsh sound. 'I might even ask you if that offer of a job is still on the cards.'

'You don't need to ask. It will always be open to you.'

'Thanks. That's nice to know.' He placed a hand on her shoulder and she peered up into his face, as if expecting more, but he let his hand slide away from her and heaved a sigh. 'Come on, I'll see you home. I need to get busy again. I have to keep working away at our problems.'

They walked along the street together, and Donovan could feel her nearness, was aware that despite the space separating their shoulders she was drawing him mentally. He wondered why she was suddenly able to exert influence on him after the years he had known her and how he'd been oblivious of any real attraction until now. They paused at the batwings, and the lamplight issuing over them bathed her face in illuminating brilliance. He caught his breath, struck by her beauty, and wondered why he had not been attracted to her before.

'I must go,' he said hurriedly. 'I have to see a man before I can go back to the doc's place.'

'I hope Joey will be OK,' she said. 'Goodnight, Jim. Perhaps I shall see you tomorrow.'

'I'll make a point of calling on you.' He touched his hat brim and turned away, leaving her gazing after him in speculation.

He walked along the sidewalk to the freight office. There was a light on downstairs. He tried the door, discovered it was locked and rapped on it with heavy knuckles. The sound echoed hollowly. There was no immediate response, but as he lifted his hand to knock again a man looked out the window. Donovan recognized Abe Williams, and signalled for him to open the door.

Williams stared at him for a moment, and just when Donovan expected a refusal, Williams nodded, turned away, and came to unlock the door.

'What the hell do you want now?' Williams demanded. 'I'm real busy. I have two wagons to get moving at dawn, and I'm behind with the paper-work.'

'That's tough,' Donovan retorted. 'I'm investigating a robbery and a murder, looking for three men who escaped from the jail and hoping to catch the man who shot my brother, so don't tell me your troubles.'

He stepped forward to enter the office but Williams kept the door pulled to.

'Open up,' Donovan rasped. 'I need to talk to you.'

'It can keep until tomorrow.'

Donovan suppressed a sigh and put his shoulder to the door, which flew inwards, knocking Williams back several feet. Williams, cursing a blue streak, recovered his balance as Donovan stepped across the threshold. He uttered an angry yell and lunged at Donovan, who met him with a solid right hand to the stomach. Williams gasped and bent over spasmodically, and then dropped to his knees as the strength fled from his legs. Donovan secured a grip on the collar of Williams' coat and hauled him upright.

'I ain't in the mood for fooling around,' Donovan said.

Williams staggered into his office and slumped in the chair behind the desk. He sat with his elbows on the desk top, his face in his hands, breathing noisily. Donovan stood menacingly at a corner of the desk, his face expressionless. After a few moments, Williams straightened and removed his hands from his face.

'What the hell do you want?' he demanded.

'Tell about your affair with Martha Preston.'

Williams' expression changed as he took in Donovan's words. He opened his mouth to deny the fact, but Donovan's face warned him that it would be futile to attempt to do so.

'How did you find out?' he countered.

'That doesn't matter. I know about it, and I need to know what was going on, so spill it.'

'It was a private matter.'

'Martha was murdered, so a secret affair could be connected to her death. Stop wasting my time and talk. Tell me about you and Martha.'

'There's nothing to tell. It ran its course and petered out.'

'That's not what I heard. You wanted to finish it and turned nasty when Martha didn't want to. So what happened? Had you found someone else? That's a pretty good motive for murder. You could have killed Martha to put an end to the affair.'

'That's a load of horse manure!' Williams grimaced. 'Don't try to pin murder on me.'

'Get down to business, Williams. It seems Martha's murder lies between you and Preston. You were the two men in her life, and Preston is the kind of man who would take his wife's disloyalty as a personal insult.'

'Then go chase him.' Williams shook his head. 'You're barking up the wrong tree here.'

'I'm not accusing you. I'm just looking at the options, and I need to hear your side of it.'

'I don't have a side. I finished with Martha more than a week ago. If anyone tells you different then it's a damn lie. Now beat it and let me get on with my work.'

Donovan stared into Williams' face, realized he would get nothing more and turned away.

'I'll do some more checking and then come back to you,' he promised.

He opened the office door. Williams followed him hurriedly and ushered him out to the street. When Donovan stepped on to the sidewalk, Williams slammed the door, and Donovan heard the key turn in the lock. He paused to consider his next move. He thought of going to see Della, but was reluctant to, and could think of no valid reason to confront Mort Preston again.

The light in Williams' office was extinguished, leaving him in deeper shadow. Donovan frowned as he looked at the darkened window. Williams reckoned he was up to his neck in work, and yet he was quitting. The freighter's footsteps sounded inside the building, and then Williams' voice rasped, the sound coming easily through the door.

'Hey, you upstairs, I'm gonna get the horses now so come and wait inside the back door.'

Williams' feet sounded again, and Donovan, his mind suddenly alive with conjecture, hastened into the side alley and ran silently through the shadows to the back lots. He halted inside the alley, blinking rapidly to accustom his eyes to the dark surroundings, and crouched down low so that the figure emerging from the building was silhouetted. It was Williams, hurrying into the freight yard.

Donovan followed at a distance, waited outside the yard and saw the yellow light of a lantern relieve the deep gloom of the private stable. A horse stamped. Williams' voice sounded as he talked to the animals inside.

Minutes later, Williams led four saddled horses out of the stable. Donovan faded back into deeper shadows as the freighter took the animals to the back door of the office. The door was opened and a mumble of voices sounded. Donovan stiffened, recognizing Elroy Johnson. His eyes had now become accustomed to the darkness and he watched as four figures emerged from the office and swung into the waiting saddles.

'Cullen,' Williams said. 'That deputy, Donovan, is a nuisance. Knock him off for me, will you?'

'I'll do it,' Johnson said. 'I'll ride along to the law office and brace him.'

'You don't have to go anywhere, Johnson,' Donovan called. 'I'm here, and ready for you.'

A shocked silence followed Donovan's call, during which he drew his gun and cocked it. The next instant, as Johnson recovered from his shock, a gun blasted, tearing the shadows apart with orange gun flame. The bullet thudded into a solid object close to Donovan, who returned fire, aiming into the centre of the flash. Then all hell broke loose. Two more guns joined in, wrecking the peace of the evening, thundering lethally. Gun flashes and spurting muzzle flame dazzled Donovan. He dropped to one knee and worked his pistol, firing rapidly.

Johnson yelled and fell out of his saddle. Another figure fell out of leather. The other two spurred their mounts and moved out fast, shooting wildly in Donovan's direction. He ducked lower so their figures were silhouetted against the lighter background of the sky, ignoring the questing lead that came at him. His gun lifted and he squeezed off a shot at the nearest rider, blinking rapidly against the flash. He saw the figure sway to the right and then tumble headlong out of the saddle. Donovan dropped flat, his index finger tight against his trigger.

The third rider twisted and brought his gun to bear, firing three desperate shots. None hit Donovan, but he felt a tug at his waist and realized his holster had been struck. He rolled over once, and saw the third rider jumping his horse forward in a desperate attempt to trample him.

A steel-shod hoof grazed Donovan's left shoulder. He rolled clear, twisting away as the rider jerked on his reins to bring the horse in closer. Donovan sprang to his feet, sidestepped the horse and launched himself at the rider. He caught hold of the man's left arm, pulled him close, and struck with his pistol, slamming the long barrel into the shadowed face. The horse whirled away. Donovan retained his hold on the man and dragged him out of the saddle.

A pistol blasted, almost in Donovan's face, the shot coming from his right. The shadows were so dense he could see no more than a faint outline. He and the outlaw he had grabbed were standing side by side. The shot missed Donovan and struck the dismounted rider, who fell in a heap. Donovan half turned quickly, throwing up his gun. He recognized the big, blocky figure of Abe Williams coming at him. Satisfaction filled him. At last Williams had come out into the open.

Donovan fired and the bullet struck Williams in

the chest. The freighter lost his hold on his gun and went over backwards. Donovan cocked his gun but it was not needed. Williams was motionless on the ground. The raucous sounds of the shooting faded quickly into the night, until only the gunsmoke remained, thick and pungent in the darkness.

Donovan kicked Williams' gun away before bending over the freighter. Williams was groaning softly. Donovan turned to the man who had collected a slug from Williams. He struck a match to illuminate an upturned face and a pang stabbed through him when he discovered that it was Cullen. The outlaw was dead. Donovan approached Elroy Johnson, who was lying on his back with Donovan's first slug in his left shoulder. Johnson was alive but unconscious. Donovan was grimly satisfied – Johnson would live to stand trial. He moved on to the third man, saw it was Noll Watson, also dead, and continued on to the rider who had been shot out of his saddle. He found Shap Kelly, who had crossed the Great Divide.

Several men were coming along the alley, moving cautiously and calling excitedly. Donovan asked one of them to bring a lamp and another to fetch the doctor. He went back to Williams' side and dropped to one knee. Williams was on his back, his face upturned to the night.

'Can you hear me, Williams?' Donovan asked softly.

'You've done for me, Donovan,' Williams replied in a low, wavering tone.

'You should have stayed out of it,' Donovan replied. 'Hold on. The doc will be here directly. Just lie still and hang on.'

'My time has come,' Williams asserted. He reached out an unsteady hand and grasped Donovan's left wrist. 'You hit me good, and I don't want to die with sin on my soul. I killed Martha but I didn't steal the money. I wouldn't have killed her but she threatened to tell Preston about us so I had to shut her mouth.'

His voice trailed away to nothing and only the sound of his laboured breathing broke the silence. Footsteps sounded in the alley, coming closer, and Donovan stood up. Doc Hardy appeared, carrying his medical bag. A townsman followed with a lantern, and a yellow glare danced over the grim scene.

'Good news for you, Jim,' Hardy said as he dropped to one knee beside Williams. 'I reckon Joey will survive. He should be right as rain in a month or so. Now, what have we got here?'

He told the man with the lamp to hold it closer and opened Williams' shirt. Donovan looked down, saw the position of the bullet wound and knew from grim experience that Williams was on the way out. Doc Hardy looked up, his face shadowed from the lamplight, his eyes glinting. He shook his head.

'He was talking to me,' Donovan said quietly. 'He said he wanted to ease his conscience.'

'You better hurry it up then.' Hardy moved back. 'He'll go at any moment.'

Donovan dropped to his knees. 'Williams,' he

called. 'You want to clear your conscience? Tell me what those outlaws were doing hiding in your place.'

Williams' eyes flickered open. He made an involuntary movement with his left hand, tried to raise it but could not, and sighed.

'I got caught up with Cullen a long time ago,' he said in a hoarse whisper. 'We were fixing to steal silver from a mine, but it fell through when you arrested Kelly. Johnson and the other two came to me for help when Art Walsh let them out of jail this evening.' His tone sharpened. 'You better watch out for Johnson, Donovan. He hates you for putting him in prison. He sneaked out of my place this evening soon as it got dark and shot your brother Joey in his cell. He killed the sheriff, too. And he told me he went into the store after I killed Martha, and robbed it. He knew Joey had seen him with the sack over his head and was afraid he could be identified. And as soon as he heard that Joey wasn't dead he said he'd go and finish him off before he rode out.'

'Johnson's past doing more devilment.' Donovan glanced to where Johnson had been lying, saw the space was empty and started to his feet; Johnson had gone. 'Where's Johnson?' he called urgently. 'Did anyone see him get up?'

There was no reply from the gathering townsmen. Donovan ran through the alley and paused on the street to look around, his thoughts on Joey. He ran toward the doctor's house, drawing his gun.

There was a lantern over the doctor's front door.

Donovan saw a lurching figure move into its radius of light and recognized Johnson. He ran faster, lifting his gun as he called his name. Johnson paused and swung around. He was holding a pistol. His left hand was pressed against his bloodied left shoulder.

Donovan cocked his gun and levelled it. He slowed to a walk twenty yards from Johnson.

'It ends here, Johnson,' Donovan called. 'I know you took money from the store after Williams killed Martha, and you shot Joey because he saw you there and you were afraid he would tell. You're holding a gun so you've got a choice – use it or throw it down.'

'You ain't putting me in prison a second time,' Johnson rasped. 'I'll see you in hell before I die.'

He lifted his pistol and thumbed back the hammer. Donovan moved simultaneously and fired. The slug hit Johnson and he was knocked back by the impact, as if he had been kicked by a mule. But he did not go down. He recovered his balance and returned fire. His first bullet smacked into Donovan's right side. Donovan went down in the dust, teeth clenched against flaring pain. He lifted his pistol, lined up the foresight on Johnson's chest and squeezed the trigger.

Johnson dropped in his tracks, jerking convulsively. He kicked until he died. Donovan sagged, loosed his hold on the gun and pressed his right hand against his hip, where he could feel the stickiness of blood. When he tried to get to his feet his right leg refused to move. He looked round. Figures were approaching, attracted by the shooting. Doc Harvey was one of the first to reach him. Donovan lay back in the dust, relieved that the gun storm was over.

Della came up and dropped to her knees at his side. She clasped his hand and he looked up into her worried face, aware that her offer of a job was the most attractive proposal he had ever received. He was sick of law dealing – trying to be in two places at once; doing his civic duty and looking after Joey. It had taken a bullet, he reflected, to knock some sense into him.

'I'll take the job, Della,' he said.

She looked keenly at him, saw determination in his eyes and nodded smilingly.

'I thought you would eventually,' she replied.

He squeezed her hand, and the action told her more than anything he could have said. His senses swirled, and as he lost consciousness he became aware of excitement filling him because of the promise of a new way of life that beckoned him.